WHEN MAYHEM MEANS MURDER

Carli Cano Mystery Series

Book 2

Maryse Laflamme

• • • ● • ● • ● • •

ISBN – Paperback: 978-1-7351721-7-0   ISBN – Ebook: 978-1-7351721-9-4

Book Cover by 100Covers.com

DEDICATION

As always, to Paul-Henri and Alexanne, my constant north stars, and to Olivia, the fiercest girl of all!

CONTENTS

UNLOCK CARLI'S EXCLUSIVE PREQUEL—ABSOLUTELY FREE!

Ever wondered why Carli ditched the Big Apple for the colorful streets of San Miguel and a fashion wonderland of her own making? The answer is juicier than you think!

Join my Insider tribe by signing up for my VIP mailing list and get exclusive access to the **prequel that spills all the matcha tea** about it! This is one backstory you can only get here because it's NOT available elsewhere and never will be!

So, grab Your Free Prequel, *Stitched in Deceit* right here: https://MaryseLaflamme.com

Who needs a decoder ring when you have the key to Carli's past? See you on the inside!

PROLOGUE

M y cell phone broke out in a dance from the front pouch of my Coach handbag. The metallic zipper brushed against my fingers as I reached in to grab it.

But it was a call I could have done without.

I frowned when I saw the name on the caller ID.

"Hola, Adele," I greeted her, trying to sound upbeat, hearing the muffled murmur of her nearby television.

"Carli!" She exclaimed, the urgency in her voice palpable.

"Wh ... what?!" I asked, my heart drumming against my chest, echoing the loud raindrops that began to tap against my window.

"He's gone!"

"Gone wh ... " But realization struck, the coldness settling in my stomach like a chunk of ice. An intense tremor ran down my spine, electrifying me.

"No! No, no, no!" Shock rippled through me.

"How?" I managed, fingers trembling, the phone's cool screen pressing against my cheek.

"Not sure. He was found bleeding ... so much blood ... on the ground ..."

The weight of her words pressed down on me, thickening the air in the room, while Dapper circled my legs, meowing.

My thoughts raced, the distant barks of a neighbor's roof dog distracting me.

"Carli?" Adele's voice cut through, sharper than the piercing notes of a nearby siren, probably on its way to the scene.

"*¿Mande?* I don't know what to say." I responded, momentarily disoriented, the sirens becoming a distant murmur.

A pause. The heavy beat of my heart filled the silence.

Then, "Someone said there's a chance he was going ..." Her voice faded away as if she was losing reception.

"Going to what?" I nearly yelled, not wanting to lose the connection, wondering if she'd been about to say what I thought she'd say. The room seemed to tilt, the faint hum of the ceiling fan above me growing more pronounced.

The gravity of the situation hit me. What tangled webs we weave.

I got a dial tone. She was gone.

I *had* to know more. Hanging up, desperate for answers, I dialed Antonio. No answer the first time, or the second. The silence between the rings felt suffocating.

On the third try, his exasperated voice came through. "Carlota! I'm in the middle of this!"

I bristled at his use of my birth name, the dim glow of a nearby streetlight filtering through my sheer curtains.

"Someone I know might be involved in this mess, Antonio!"

"And I'm here with my team trying to get to the bottom of it, you blowing up my phone is not helping."

He hung up on me.

But this happened much later. First came everything that led to it ...

Chapter 1

I strolled down the streets of Centro in San Miguel de Allende, my hometown, quiet joy in my heart over the pleasant Friday evening ahead, my mind miles away from the nefarious doings about to unleash into my life.

I'd almost reached my favorite fourth cousin's restaurant, Manuel's Eatery, appreciative of the crisp, but mild late April evening, enjoying the relative quiet of the town after the recent festivities of Holy Week.

But then, like a cold gust in the middle of summer, a memory from yesterday hit me, and my high spirits plummeted.

It wasn't so much what I saw, but *who* I saw. And with whom.

I shook it off in favor of enjoying the moment.

The architecture of the buildings in the streets of Centro, the center of the town where all the celebrations took place and where most tourists spent their time, always lifted my spirits, so I focused on that. Each building, a symphony of color—from the vibrant yellows and warm ochres to myriad shades of history, artwork gleaming in gallery windows, colorful clothing worn by tourists and locals alike.

But it wasn't all bright and cheery. Every so often, like a shadow amongst the light, the less fortunate would silently seat themselves on the sidewalks, hands or clear plastic cups reaching out in quiet hope.

Like Alma. In her usual spot, she was wrapped in a serape that danced with green, blue, orange, and red, her face brown like a mango past its sell-by-date. Wrinkles as deep as canyons, each a testament to a harsh life. I crossed the street to her, and handed her a note instead of dropping it in her cup.

Her eyes, crinkled and laser-like, met mine, a thank you shining from hers, though with a desperation stamp like a watermark behind them. She gave me her trademark, nearly toothless, smile. My heart cracked, while her simple mumbled *gracias* lifted my mood.

Despite my love for the beauty, and the posh lifestyle available in San Miguel, abject poverty colored its periphery like a dark cloud, a reminder that it could happen to any of us, were it not for sheer luck, or the blessing of God. I was taught at an early age to not take it for granted. I saw helping those like Alma as both a responsibility and a pleasure.

I re-crossed the street and entered Manuel's restaurant. As soon as I stepped through the door, my shoulders melted downwards, and the crease between my eyes eased, while the tension in my jaw released. The ambient lighting bathed the space in a gentle glow, reflecting off the polished surfaces and creating a calm atmosphere.

This place!

I stood in the entrance a moment, breathing deeply, taking it all in.

Always, this place energized and lulled me into relaxation at the same time. My gaze instinctively traveled to the main dining room's back wall, composed of tan stone sourced directly from our family's sprawling estate, Hacienda del Cielo Azul. I helped Manuel collect some of those. Looking at the wall felt like stepping into a memory—the rustic scent of our family fields in my nostrils, and the silhouettes of our childhood homes appearing in my mind's eye.

The stone wall stood out in contrast to the other three, which were painted a bright sunflower-yellow, and mostly covered by colorful artwork on loan from Fábrica La Aurora—once a textile factory, but now home to various artists' studios. The paintings were a burst of colors, featuring yellows, reds, blues, and even more, and showcased scenes from San Miguel and other Mexican towns.

Sleek modern furniture coupled with the artwork gave the space a chic bohemian feel. Latin world tunes played, occasionally punctuated by a spirited Flamenco number. The melodies swirled around, but never intruded, the volume's level allowing diners to savor their conversations along with the music. Add to that murmurs from the bar, the soft clink of cutlery, and it all blended into a familiar symphony that spelled comfort to me.

That is, until the faint hum of laughter and clinking glasses from the bar—which lined the entire length of the wall on the left of the entrance, reached me. Then, amidst the bar's patrons, I spotted Lisa Martin and her husband, John Sullivan. But, worse, is that she saw me.

"Carli!" She called out, her voice slicing through the soft melodies of the music and the general noise of the restaurant.

I nodded to them in greeting and gave my best I-can't-stop-to-talk-right-now smile, signaling I wasn't up for a chat, hoping it would satisfy her. She waved me over anyway. My heart sank.

Did I go to her because I wanted to be subjected to her underhanded way of trying to get information out of me about that fateful day six months ago? No. Did I want to hear her gossip that usually entailed dishing others' secrets? No. But could I avoid it? Also, no.

First, in true Lisa style, she wouldn't let up, this much I knew. She'd come get me, her steps determined, and bring me back to the bar with her if need be so she could try a new tactic to loosen my lips.

As a regular consignor in my women's designer clothing resale shop, Carli's Secret Closet, it would be rude to refuse her. When one lived in a smaller town such as this, especially within the bosom of the expat community, nearly everyone knew everyone else, at least by sight. Or by rumor. And I didn't need her to start false rumors about me.

I lived with one foot in the expat community, and the other in the Mexican locals' world, my large Mexican family all around me.

I had split my time growing up between Austin, with my grandparents from my late bio-father's side, and San Miguel. I'd also soaked up three years in New York City, and I confidently blended the Austin drawl with Manhattan hustle in my English. And Spanish? I spoke it with the authenticity of a native because that's exactly what I was.

I'd still be in The Big Apple, though, were it not for that thing that happened, well, more than a "thing," but in the end, I'd found my way back to San Miguel to create my own fashion and design queendom, the kind that suited me best, the one I ruled over like a queen bee.

For me, fashion wasn't just business. It was the magic of making any woman, regardless of size or shape, feel like her most beautiful and confident self in the perfect dress. And to do it with designer vintage dresses as often as possible. I loved, loved, loved, loved, *loved*, helping her find garments that made her shine.

Dealing with tricky customers, like Lisa, could dampen my enthusiasm, but they were few. In the end, Lisa probably had good intentions. She just couldn't keep a secret and loved juicy tales—which she shared with no restraint, often embellishing them. But something about her set off my internal alarms. And life had shown me the value of heeding those warnings.

Another twist about running into Lisa and John? I had seen John just the day before in an unexpected location in town and with someone he probably should not have been with. I'd made an about face then, but wasn't sure if he'd noticed me.

I approached the bar. "*Hola* Lisa," I said, "*Hola* John."

We all did the cheek kissy thing and Lisa wasted no time digging in.

"So, still can't talk about it, eh?" Said Lisa, excitement in her voice, impatience in her eyes.

Did she not realize she was talking about real people, real-*now-dead* people she'd known? Socialized with?

"No, I cannot." I met her gaze head-on, challenging her silently.

She held my stare just as intently, without blinking.

Finally, she responded. "Well, yes, of course, you're right." Her eyes shifted to the left, a telltale sign of someone attempting to fathom a perspective foreign to her own.

Disappointment oozed from her. I pretended to not notice.

John squinted in my direction, a hint of curiosity in his eyes. Then, with a casual shrug, he turned his attention back to his drink, taking a deliberate sip. He often distanced himself from Lisa's gossip. At social events, she'd flit from person to person gathering tidbits like a bird building a nest, adding to her vast library of gossip. He'd simply stay in his seat and chat with his neighbors.

I grabbed the seconds of awkward silence remaining before she thought of something else to say. "Well, I'm meeting friends for dinner. I hope you both enjoy your evening."

"Alright, Carli. It was nice seeing you." Lisa said, her longing for what I wouldn't tell her visible on her face.

"Carli, always a pleasure," added John, turning my way again.

"Thank you, *hasta luego*." See you later.

I leaned toward Lisa first for the obligatory goodbye cheek pecks, and then, because it would have been rude not to, I pecked John's cheeks too.

As I walked away, what I'd seen yesterday came back to me.

What might it mean?

CHAPTER 2

J ust as I turned my back to the bar and faced the dining room, I saw my cousin Antonio standing at the entrance to the largest of four alcoves—which created small, semi-private dining rooms—that lined the right wall of the restaurant. I waved, smiled, and headed his way.

"Hola Antonio!" I said in greeting once I reached the table, happy to see him.

"Chica!" Girl. He opened his arms wide and pulled me into a hug.

"You look beautiful. As always." Said Antonio.

More cheek pecks.

He looked toward the bar, a pensive look on his face, having obviously noticed that I'd just been talking to John and Lisa.

He'd been about to say something, but Manuel, whom I'd spotted approaching us from the entrance to the kitchen in the far back, grabbed me by the waist, turned me toward him and kissed my cheek before letting go.

"*¡Oye! Vato!*" Said Antonio. "I saw her first!" He added, tongue in cheek.

"I don't think so," said Manuel, his face overtaken by a huge smile. "I met her when I was about two or three days old, *sabes?*" You know.

"Nobody remembers that far back," argued Antonio, rolling his eyes.

These two could never stop their endless compulsion to compete. The same childish banter, over and over. Who'd believe that Antonio was the Sargento de Investigación (detective sergeant) for the city of San Miguel? Or that Manuel owned this beautiful, "It" place of a restaurant, with dozens of glowing features in all the important magazines, and long lists of five-star online reviews on all the important review sites?

"No, but there are historical records to prove it," retorted Manuel, making me laugh.

"Ah! Can I see those?" Asked Antonio, a smirk on his face.

"They're *oral* records, *vato*. *Mi mama*, and *mi abuela* told me the story a thousand times."

"Yes, my mother and grandmother too," I added, a grin on my own face, getting into it.

Antonio gave me disappointed puppy eyes. How could I betray him? They seemed to say. How could I take Manuel's side? But, as the thousand other times, okay, a bit of an exaggeration, we'd repeated a similar routine, it was all in jest.

I gave him my "for real?" look and he grinned.

"Where's Adele?" I asked Antonio.

"Mexico City. Business," he replied, his lips drooping for a moment.

I pouted on his behalf. He liked her here in San Miguel, but the woman had a business to run, one that took her out of town frequently. Those homes weren't going to decorate themselves.

Adele, Antonio's new-ish girlfriend, was a gorgeous blonde fit for a Vogue cover. From our first meeting, I knew she'd eventually show up at my shop, Carli's Secret Closet. And when she did, she immediately became a part of my unofficial fashionista tribe.

Now, finally, I sat and placed my Louis Vuitton Scala mini pouch on the hook beneath the table, just to the right of me.

I didn't hesitate to sip wine and get lost in the beat of the music, to feel the warmth of being with close friends, with family. Because, ultimately, the past is a ghost, one I preferred not to summon. Life was meant to be lived today, not in the past. Why be chained to bygones?

Just as the server left our table, Luna, my closest childhood friend, appeared at the entrance to our private space.

At age seven, Luna and I had locked eyes over melting vanilla and strawberry scoops at an ice cream parlor our dads had unknowingly chosen to take us to at the same time. The moment glued us together, making us lifelong partners on life's rollercoaster. We poured our grief into one another, weathered storms, and basked in sunlight and joy together. As needed. And sometimes over vanilla and strawberry ice cream.

Now, as she stood in front of us, our jaws all dropped, even mine, though I'd known what she'd be wearing because she'd gotten her dress at my shop last week, and my seamstresses had altered it to fit her like a glove. It's the accessories she'd added to complete her outfit that had me gaping in delight.

Luna, tall like a palm but with the girth of an oak, elevated big and beautiful to a whole new level. And her style? Bold, vibrant—no blending into the background for her. She held the place of star fashionista in my book.

Tonight, she'd plopped a Jackie Kennedy pill hat on her head, and wore a vintage A-line Dior ball gown with a short cape collar adorned with three flowers made of the same fabric as the dress. She'd had the gown shortened so no one could miss the pink and see-through four-inch-heel Christian Louboutins with their red soles and a multitude of straps around her ankles. Toeless, so of course, she sported purple polish on her toes. You'd think a five-foot nine woman would wear flats or shorter heels, but no. She dressed how she liked, and relished the attention.

Luna worked from home as an in high-demand web developer, so whenever she left her house, she liked celebrating by dressing up. Over the top. Always.

To complete this look, she carried an iconic Elisa Petit Modèle handbag—patent leather and embroidered fabric of red, blue, yellow, white, with touches of orange and black. We'd be blinded were it not for the fact that her dress and hat were both full bubblegum pink. On anyone else, this would look garish. On Luna? Sublime! She looked like a work of art.

Now, we all stood, surrounded her, hugged her, did the kissy thing all over again, as people in the restaurant craned their necks to look at this apparition.

"Oh, *mis amores,*" she gushed, channeling Lauren Bacall's sultry and smoky voice. My loves.

"Wait, you look so bright, let me get my sunglasses," said Manuel, patting his pockets, grinning, which earned him a soft punch to the shoulder from Luna, though her huge smile took away any pain, no doubt.

"Manuel, Manuel, Manuel ... if Carli and Antonio didn't like you so much ..." The scent of her perfume, both sweet and spicy, intensified as she drew closer. She tilted her head and squinted at him as if trying to figure out the best way to hurt him.

We all laughed as this was often their usual first exchange.

"Okay, let's all sit. We're causing a commotion," said Manuel, looking around his bustling restaurant, conversations from other tables reaching us, the scent of food making me deeply hungry as servers walked nearby, their arms laden with plates filled with chicken *mole* and other delicacies from the menu. We were all standing just outside the alcove, blocking the way.

We all sat.

I picked up my glass of wine and held it high toward the center of the table. The others did the same.

"Salud!" I called out. Cheers.

"Salud" they all countered.

We took our first sips. It felt delicious to be here in the company of such good friends.

"Hmmm ... this *wine*!" Said Luna, her eyes rolling in her head.

She proposed another toast. "To Manuel, the best wine chooser in the whole world!"

We all laughed and clinked our glasses once more.

"I guess it helps that the man owns a restaurant with a magnificent wine cellar," she added, winking at him.

"Yes, it does help him," quipped Manuel, chuckling.

This made us all erupt in laughter again.

Manuel and Luna began to catch up on one another's lives, and Antonio took the opportunity to ask me about my stop at the bar.

"I saw you say hello to John and Lisa," he said in a low voice, his eyes intense on me.

CHAPTER 3

"Yes. So?" I asked, surprised to hear him bring that up.

"Nothing. Just that there might be trouble there. John Sullivan was seen around, outside Centro, a few times. Always with a certain *señorita.* One with three brothers we keep an eye on." He raised his eyebrows twice in quick succession.

I blinked, and stared at Antonio, glancing at the others to see if they'd heard. But now, Luna was dissecting the menu while Manuel ran commentary on every choice available, like a proud papa showing off his children.

"That John Sullivan?" I asked under my breath, feigning ignorance, pointing my thumb backward toward the bar, but Manuel and Luna both snapped their heads around to us anyway.

"¿Mande?" What. Asked Luna, eyes traveling between Antonio and me, her wine glass halfway to her mouth.

Manuel dropped his chin, and raised his eyebrows at us, now also intrigued.

"John Sullivan and a, uh ... a certain *señorita*," I said, shaking my head and looking from Manuel to Luna.

Luna, never shy, bent over backwards trying to see John Sullivan at the bar.

"Ah well, he's not the first expat to rob a cradle for one of our young beauties. We can only hope this one had her *Quinceañera* (girl's celebration of her transition to womanhood at age 15) a few years back, rather than, say, last week." She looked pensive for a moment, then asked Antonio, "Are you sure?"

Before he could answer, I said "I'm sure it must be him."

They turned in unison to look at me as if their heads shared the same swivel. They waited. I ran my fingers through my hair. I sighed, deep and long.

"Let's keep it between us, okay?" I asked, looking each in the eye in turn. They all nodded, Antonio, his gaze hooded. I paused to take a sip of water.

"I saw them too. Yesterday, actually. In *Los Mezquites*." I set my glass down, biting my lower lip at the same time.

Saying it made me sad. What was John Sullivan getting himself into? Our exchanged glances were like scattered marbles, directionless, everyone surprised at this turn in the conversation.

Antonio took a deep breath. "Two of her brothers we know for sure are *halcones*—falcons and the other we suspect just moved up ranks to *sicario* (hitman)," he shared, his gaze sinking deep into his wine, swirling it contemplatively, lost in the gravity of his revelation.

Luna and I exchanged a quick glance before turning to stare at him. What did that mean?

"What ... what does a *halcón* do again, and a *sicario*?" Luna asked. She picked up her wine, but put it back down without taking a sip. "I don't follow those things," she added.

"A *halcón*'s job is to watch us so they can tell their *capo*—drug lord—what the police is up to. They're the lowest position in the organization." He leaned in, elbows on the table. "A *sicario* on the other hand ..." He sighed, shaking his head back and forth, slowly, pursing his lips.

"Well?" Asked Luna, leaning forward herself.

"A *sicario* ... well, to put it bluntly, a *sicario* carries out assassinations, kidnappings, extortions, protections."

"Oh ..." Luna said. Her eyes narrowed and she moved farther back into her chair, clasping her hands together on the table.

None of us spoke after that, as if observing silence in memoriam of those murdered by cartels the world over.

Antonio leaned in, cutting through the lingering silence. "And it looks like there's a hit out on one of them." He paused, scanning our faces to make sure he had our full attention. We must have looked as if about to ask for details.

He put up both hands like stop signs. "I can't say more than that. And I'm only telling you this much because you all seem interested in this now," he continued, taking a sip of his water, "and I don't want any of you to be get caught in any crossfire of any kind." He set down his glass with a slight thud.

"*¿Entiendes?*" He jabbed a finger at each of us emphasizing the urgency of his words, and resting on me longer than on the others.

"But ... but, what? Someone is supposed to kill him, is what you mean, Antonio?" Luna asked, leaning closer in his direction, fascination and horror on her face in equal proportions.

I whipped my head Antonio's way, waiting for him to respond.

Before he could, Manuel, evidently tired of the gloomy talk, twirling a napkin between his fingers, said, "Well, *hola*, did we come here, to *my* restaurant, to be depressed?"

He slapped the napkin down on the table, raising his chin like a lord demanding respect from his subjects. "The *cartel* guy should get whatever's coming to him. And John Sullivan should stay away from those kinds of people, and take care of his own self." This, he whispered, considering the man himself was sitting just yards away from us in this very restaurant, *his* restaurant, spending money.

"Our job tonight is to enjoy this dinner we're about to have," he continued. He gestured expansively at the table. "I planned it, slaved over it all day, and now I want to enjoy it with my friends." He picked up his wine glass. "My smiling, laughing, *happy* friends. *Sí?*" He took a sip, then placed the glass back down with a deliberate thud. His eyes traveled around the table, stopping for a moment on each of us in turn, a twinkle in them.

"Slaved all day. *Really?*" Asked Antonio, his skeptical face on full display.

Manuel laughed out loud.

Luna asked, "Don't you have sous-chefs to do all the cutting? And the cooking? I mean, who's cooking now?"

She extended her arm to show all the diners in the main room that couldn't have been waiting on him to return to the kitchen.

Manuel, Antonio, and I chuckled.

"Sí," said Antonio. "This *vato* hardly works, as far as I know," he added.

"¿Mande? Me? *I* don't work?" Asked Manuel, his hackles up over this pronouncement.

"Alright, no fighting tonight." I pointed to each of them in turn.

They both turned to me, looking insulted, and said—in unison, "We're not fighting."

Luna and I locked eyes in glee. And then, just in time to stop my cousins from continuing their competitive banter—which could last for hours sometimes—the server appeared to ask if we were ready to eat.

While the others placed their orders, my thoughts drifted to John. His good looks, the definition of tall, dark, and handsome, except he was blond, could captivate younger hearts.

How would Lisa handle whispers about her husband's apparent philandering? She, the gossip queen, the tables turned on her?

San Miguel had little room for hiding an illicit affair, even if the man never brought his young mistress to the usual expat hangouts. Word traveled fast!

What could become more troublesome, though, was *La Señorita*'s cartel-affiliated brothers.

What if they discovered he was married already? And, therefore, could have no good intentions regarding their sister?

Or raised eyebrows at the pronounced age gap I'd noticed the day before? There could be only one interpretation in their eyes.

Did John Sullivan even grasp the perilous web he was entangled in?

CHAPTER 4

I woke up early the next day to find Dap sitting on my chest, in sphinx pose, his green eyes intense on my face.

I yawned. "Dap, *mi amor*, you know I don't like that," I said with little enthusiasm.

Meow was his response. Of course.

I closed my eyes again, while I petted his sleek black coat interrupted only by four white paws, feeling the soft rhythm of his heartbeat against my hand.

When I'd rescued him, his black coat and white paws had captured my heart, evoking Roaring Twenties' dapper gents in snazzy suits and two-toned shoes. So, I named him Dapper, but affectionately called him Dap. When he got into mischief, though, he became *Dapper da Cat Garcia Cano*.

I slid him aside, feeling the warmth he left behind on the sheet. Sitting on the edge of the bed, I reached for my robe, an as soft-as-can-be full-length red cashmere I'd ecstatically snapped up for myself when a consignor had brought it in. Its rich color reminded me of ripe cherries in the summer sun.

Dap knew the morning routine. His soft, rhythmic purring accompanied me as we went to the kitchen. Here began my sacred morning ritual of making the first cup of matcha tea for the day.

First, fill the electric kettle with purified water, set it to heat to the one-hundred-seventy-five degrees a perfect cup of matcha green tea required. My friends and family laughed about the kettle I'd brought home from Texas because it had temperature settings for all sorts of teas. But what other kind of kettle could a girl have if she wanted that perfect cup each time? I just didn't understand people who didn't understand that.

As I waited for the water to heat up, the gentle humming of the kettle filling the air, I gazed out my second story kitchen window, at the garden of the home just behind mine.

Velvety pink bougainvillea cascaded down our communal wall, their scent occasionally gracing the air.

Beyond this vibrant curtain, the Gonzalez's backyard echoed *El Charco del Ingenio*, a well-known botanical garden with rare cacti just outside of San Miguel. I'd never have those prickly beauties in my own garden, but cherished looking at theirs.

The kettle chirped, alerting me the water was ready, steam dancing upwards, ghostlike. I poured some into my favorite large, rounded, flowered ceramic mug to heat it, while I measured the ingredients for my concoction into a blender jar. Matcha powder, various mushroom powders, earthy and rich, promising to boost my immune system, pungent ashwagandha, and astragalus, with its subtle, woody scent.

Add to that a tablespoon of coconut oil, its aroma transporting me to sunny beaches, and one golden tablespoon of raw honey from my family's hacienda. I couldn't get this concoction anywhere in the world outside my kitchen.

I blended the whole for ten seconds. *Aqui!* One perfect morning beverage for me.

This morning's ritual, though, felt tinged with an unsettling undertone, a subtle shift in life's energy I couldn't quite grasp. Everything seemed askew, like a painting slightly off its hook. Unexpectedly, John Sullivan's face intruded into my thoughts, and what Antonio had said.

But I let it go, because, as usual, at this point in the ritual, Dap meowed at my feet. Rolling my eyes playfully, I tossed him three salmon treats. He gobbled them up and dashed ahead, racing me to the rooftop—a shift from his old habit of tailing me. *Gato loco*! Crazy cat.

Once on the roof, I kept my eyes on my favorite chair, plopped myself into it, and placed the matcha potion on the table next to me. I then took a deep breath, closed my eyes a moment to feel and smell the air, to listen to the early morning noises of *Centro*, quieter now than they'd be the rest of the day and into the late evening.

Just then, roof dogs kicked off a barking spree. This always startled newcomers, but for locals, it meshed with cars honking, occasional mariachi tunes, firecrackers, and church bells. Lifting my eyes, I caught the crown jewel of views—the Parroquia's pink spires rising above the boutiques and eateries huddled around it, as if cozying up to a winter fire.

Dap basked in a sunbeam. All that in order, I savored the first sip of my tea.

My thoughts wandered back to las night again. John Sullivan. I mean, why? He and Lisa owned a beautiful home in Ventanas de San Miguel, an upscale development, and an apartment in Toronto for when they visited. Had he loved Lisa at one time? Did he still have feelings for her despite his slip-up? They had a nice lifestyle. Why risk it for a fling?

Especially for a fling with someone who had a brother in the cartel with a contract on his head. Did John realize the danger he faced? Shouldn't someone tell him?

My pocket vibrated. I pulled out my phone and looked at a text message. Manuel.

> Can you talk?

> Sure

The phone rang, and I picked up.

"Hola, Primo!" Hello, cousin. I greeted him.

"Hi, cousin!" He said back to me.

We'd played this game since we were children, him, and I. If I greeted him in Spanish, he greeted me in English, and vice versa.

"Dinner was so nice last night, Manuel! *Muchos gracias* once again." Thank you so much.

"I'd planned to call you as soon as I got done with my matcha." I added, not wanting him to think me ungrateful that he had to call me first after hosting such a fabulous dinner for us.

"Ah, yes. The morning matcha."

I could hear the smile in his voice, as he continued: "It's nothing. What's the point of owning a restaurant if you can't feed your favorite people every now and then?"

Dear, generous Manuel. I couldn't believe what I'd once thought him capable of ...

Manuel was now going on about something in the restaurant that morning, and my mind drifted to John and the cartel, and the possibly soon-dead brother of *La Señorita*. Something needed to be done about all this mayhem.

"Hola, earth to Carli!" Called out Manuel.

"Oh, *lo siento*." Sorry. "Daydreaming about my shop." No need to bring up John Sullivan and cartel brothers' drama yet one more time.

"Are you sure, Carlita?" said Manuel, tweaking my birth name of Carlota, which I allowed no one, except my parents, to use.

I mean, my mother had named me that because she liked the name, sure: Carlota Maria Garcia Cano.

She didn't name me after the ill-fated Carlota of Mexico, who alongside her husband, Archduke Maximilian, had had their grand Mexican dreams crash and burn, after which she lost her mind. But who wanted to share a name with such a tragic figure in history?

Manuel, though? He had this knack. By swapping just one vowel, turning "Carlota" into "Carlita," he transformed it into an endearing gesture. It felt special, as long as it was just him using it, that is.

Now, he made clear the reason for his early morning call.

"I just want to be sure you don't get any ideas like approaching Sullivan. I know how you are. Antonio brought it up, too. After the last time, I hope you learned, Carli."

"Of *course*, I'm not going to approach him about it. Why would I do that? It's not my business." I asked, as innocently as I could while my face nearly set itself on fire from embarrassment, as if he'd read my thoughts.

"Maybe I never said, Carlita, but I'm very proud of the life you made here for yourself. You left that bunch of hyenas back in New York, and created everything you have here on your own." I heard him sigh, and waited him out. "Not many people can see their own lives so clearly, or be brave enough to take it in that direction when they do. I know you don't want to mess that up. *¿Verdad?*" Right.

"Aww, Manuel. Gracias. And of course, I'm not going to have anything to do with John Sullivan's business. I took in a sharp breath as if offended at the thought. "Or his girlfriend's brother's *cartel*. Sheesh." I blushed in what felt like a deep crimson, similar to the vibrant flowers on the bougainvillea on my back wall.

Of course, if I'd known then what was to come, I couldn't have faked innocence if my life had depended on it, and blushing would be the last thing I'd worry about.

CHAPTER 5

"Carliiiita ... I *know* you!"

"Manuel, stop it. I'm not going to do anything that has anything to do with any cartel men. Especially not when one of them has a contract on his head. I'm not *stupida*!" Stupid.

Manuel remained silent on the other end.

"Alright, well ... I'll see you tomorrow, I guess." He seemed unconvinced.

"Sí, of course. I'll pick up the champagne today, and make fresh orange juice before you get here. Don't come 'til ten, okay?"

"You'll play lazy and stay in bed late?" He asked.

"Yes, *vato*. Leave me alone about it. See you *mañana*!" I hung up before he could continue to grill me about John Sullivan.

His voice tinged with hidden yearning—did he fantasize about lazy mornings with me? A fantasy we couldn't indulge in. Our families' old-school stance was a roadblock for sure.

No marrying cousins, even fourth cousins like us. Legal in Mexico, maybe, but taboo in our clan—unless we rebelled.

It would mean severing family ties, our parents ashamed and disgraced. And no doubt we'd have to leave San Miguel, our hearts aching for what we'd lose—my treasured boutique, Manuel's dream restaurant. Would our love endure or crumble under the strain?

Since I also loved my family, my business, and San Miguel ...

If it was just San Miguel, could I leave? Because, besides my family being here, I sometimes wondered if it wasn't that the city had been built on a bedrock of rose quartz—which drew a lot of artists of all stripes, as well as healers—that drew me here, that made me want to stay.

When we didn't go for Sunday *comida* (lunch) at the hacienda, the place overrun by cousins, aunts, and uncles, we often had our own small brunch on my rooftop.

I'd decided to skip tomorrow's *comida*, since my parents were in Guadalajara, because my *papá* managed our renowned Hacienda del Cielo Azul tequila distillery with Manuel's dad and it needed his attention, while my shop demanded my attention later in the day. I was beginning to think it was time to start closing on Sundays. The shop was doing well enough now to afford that.

I yearned for the embrace of the hacienda, the home of my heart, and decided to do a quick weekday visit as soon as my parents returned.

Skipping the family gathering—which would take place at Manuel's parents' house—would allow me to luxuriate in a late wake-up. I'd savor my first cup of matcha, and then dive into a good book or I'd sketch. All this before Manuel arrived to grace my kitchen with his culinary magic.

Even after ditching New York's cutthroat fashion scene—I still designed clothes. Managed by a head seamstress with two assistants, my local team crafted my designs, which I sold to posh stores across Centro. My own boutique specialized in vintage couture, but some of my original pieces made the cut when they matched the vibe.

Thinking of that, I had a business to run, and couldn't linger with these thoughts or with trying to solve John and Lisa's marital problems. Or John's possible cartel complications.

I took the last sip of my tea and prepared to go downstairs to dress and head to my shop. But my phone rang again. I looked at the display. Luna.

"Hey Luna, *¿Qué onda?"* I said as I answered the call. What's up.

"Carli, you'll never believe who I just saw," Luna blurted out in her typical fashion, her voice tinged with urgency.

My heart rate quickened. "I don't want to guess. Just spill, *chica*. Who?"

"Your John Sullivan, you know, from Manuel's *restaurante*. And not alone. He was with a woman, but I don't think it's that *señorita* you were talking about because this one's at least mid-thirties. And guess what?"

"Luna, I don't want to guess. And he's not 'my' John Sullivan, hello?" She was making me impatient. I just wanted the information so I could stop gripping my phone and take a breath.

She continued. "They were having a very hot argument." And here she started whispering though I didn't know why. "Like, very hot."

The way she said "very hot" carried a weight that sank into my stomach. Luna, despite her showy ways, wasn't one to make a big deal out of nothing. That last sip of matcha sat in my throat, feeling less grounding and more like thick mud.

"Oh wow, are you *sure* it was him?" I asked, even though I knew Luna wouldn't mistake someone so easily.

"Yes, it's the man you pointed to at the restaurant. I grabbed some breakfast at that cute café by Parque Juárez, so I decided to walk around the park for a change, and there they were along the path. They got quiet when they saw me, and just started right up again as soon as I passed them." Here she finally took a breath. "I'd say it doesn't look good, *chica*. He looked furious, and the woman—well, she looked furious, too ..."

My mind began to churn. John's image, which had mysteriously clouded my thoughts earlier, resurfaced, and was now accompanied by an unsettling sense of dread.

"Could you hear what they said?" I waited, full of curiosity.

"No, I told you. They stopped talking as I got closer and didn't pick up again until I was well past them."

My hands tightened even more around the phone.

"Luna, be careful. I hope you made sure they can't hear you talking about them?"

I sensed her stiffening, and she waited a beat to answer.

"Carli, what do you take me for? First off, I'm out of the park now, and don't you think I know better?" She sounded offended, and like she was disappointed in me for thinking less of her.

"Lo siento, but you would say the same to me." Sorry.

She sighed. "I know, you're right. Okay, gotta go. I want to get home and get to work."

We said our goodbyes and hung up.

The tension that had subtly colored my morning ritual now burst into full bloom. My thoughts circled back to Manuel's warning about not getting involved with this John Sullivan thing, about the cartels. A shiver ran down my spine. What was John Sullivan tangled up in? And now *another* woman in his life? Just what was the man thinking?

Dap, sensing the shift in my mood, jumped onto my lap and looked up, his green eyes filled with feline concern. I petted him absentmindedly, grateful for the warm comfort he provided.

The phone call had succeeded in pulling me from my sacred routine and into an unsettling spiral. I sighed, gazing up at the spires of the Parroquia as if seeking divine guidance.

My gut told me this wasn't the last I'd be hearing of John Sullivan, and cartels, and mistresses. That must be why I kept thinking about his situation when it had nothing to do with me.

What I didn't know yet was just how deep current troubles ran in my town, how many people it would affect, entangling me in a web of secrets and danger.

Chapter 6

The ten-minute walk from my home to my store on Calle de Canal allowed me to take in the scene of a beautiful early spring morning. No breeze, glorious sunshine, and sixty-eight degrees.

Reaching the courtyard of my shop, I paused at the coffee cart run by a young couple, and got tea.

Grabbing my cup, I quickly unlocked my shop, and locked it right back up again to prepare for the day. As always, I turned on the sound system, set to a relaxing but uplifting Latin beat, dialed the lights to the perfect intensity, made sure the dressing rooms were in order, candles by the register and in the small restroom burning and infusing the air with their vanilla scent.

Just as I unlocked the door for business, the windchime above it tinkled like miniature steel drums. Loved the sound. That tinkling meant business!

I looked to the door, and grinned as wide as my mouth allowed.

"Adele!"

"Carli!"

We hugged and kissed hello.

"So nice to see you, girl." I said, happy to see Antonio's new girlfriend.

Adele consigned clothes to me, and today, she held three large shopping bags.

"I thought you went to the big city?" I said, glancing at the bag, which were near overflowing.

"Oh, yes. I drove back super early this morning."

"Ah, *bueno* (good). We missed you at dinner last night."

"I'm aware. I wanted to get back in time, but I had a dinner there with two clients."

"El Café? *Por favor?*" She asked.

I glanced at my cup of matcha, and thought for a moment. Sofia, my morning salesgirl would arrive shortly. Maybe Adele knew about John Sullivan ...

"As soon as Sofia arrives, we *vamos!*" We go. I said, playfully mimicking her typical blend of Spanish and English, making her chuckle.

She gave me a smile to rival Luna's, the biggest *smiler* on the face of the earth.

As if on cue, Sofia breezed in with her usual bright energy.

"Hola Carli, *hola* Adele," she called out in her singsong voice.

"Hey girl," replied Adele. "Ready to face the hordes of women who want to dazzle by wearing something special from Carli's Secret Closet?" She asked, voice filled with enthusiasm.

"Always, they all need us!" replied Sofia, grinning.

"Hey, they can be beautiful as they are!" I exclaimed.

Adele tilted her head, a mischievous glint in her eyes. "Well, in the eyes of the beholder and all that, but they look more beautiful after you've gotten your hands on their wardrobe!"

Sofia and I both laughed at that. Some truth in there. I prided myself on just that. Any woman could be beautiful if she understood how to bring forward her own best attributes by knowing which clothes to wear and how.

"Sofia, I'm leaving for a bit. Call if you need help."

Adele and I strolled along Canal Street to El Café, and once seated on its back patio, the distant hum of city life beyond the walls of the courtyard reaching us, I turned our discussion toward affairs of the heart, especially that of married people cheating. I sensed a shift in the air, the weight of secrets about to be told.

Adele stopped, iced Frappuccino with a huge dollop of whipped cream halfway to her lips.

"Are you talking about John Sullivan?" She asked, her eyes sparkling, the skin around them crinkling, her voice at near-whisper level.

A couple at the next table seemed intent on diving into one another's eyes, their hands meeting halfway across the table, entwined. I decided they presented no danger as far as spreading our conversation to others. From the sketchpads on their table, I guessed they were students at the Instituto Allende, where artists from all over the world came to learn, or perfect, their craft.

I turned back to Adele. So. She knew. I relaxed, ready to hear what she could tell me.

"Well, yes, how did you know?" I asked.

She frowned and smirked at me at the same time. The warm afternoon sunlight highlighted a mischievous glint in her eyes. She'd told me, when we'd first met, that little happened in the expat world here that she didn't know. Her maid was friends with many other maids and attended the same church. Yes, they gossiped.

I gave her my best crooked smile.

"Tsk! Carli, Carli, Carli!"She repeated my name singsong style, her voice dancing above the murmur of the other patrons in the courtyard.

"What?" I pretended innocence.

"What do you already know?" Adele asked, her head dipping to her right.

I chuckled.

"Just that I saw him in Los Mezquites with a young *señorita* the other day. And I'm not talking about the part with the million-dollar houses."

Antonio wouldn't tell me her name, so I'd have to go on dubbing her *La Señorita*. She and her brothers apparently lived in their family house in Los Mezquites. This neighborhood was a mix of luxury homes and simpler dwellings, creating a blend of wealth, modesty, and poverty. My seamstress's family had lived there for generations, making an honest living. But *La Señorita*'s cartel brothers? Apparently, no.

She nodded her head, as though I were confirming something for her.

"You know about her brothers?" She leaned toward me, lowering her voice, and the subtle scent of her sweet perfume wafted over me.

"Yes," I said, recalling Antonio's hushed warnings. "Antonio said."

"Ah, and how *is* our detective sergeant?"

"Good! He has a new girlfriend. Well, new-ish." I retorted, irreverently. "It surprises me that *she's* asking *me* how *he* is," I added.

She laughed. "Just kidding. We talked last night. And this morning." She blushed, looking down at her cup and toying with her straw.

Gazing at her with a smile, I realized she might just be "The One" for my second-favorite cousin, and I wholeheartedly approved. But still, I pivoted the conversation back to where I wanted it.

"What do you know about those brothers of hers?" I asked, back in inquisitive investigator mode.

"Cartel," was all she said. All that needed to be said. So, she knew this, too.

"And you know that one of them has a contr..."

She interrupted me, nodding. "Sí, Antonio told me that, too."

We looked at one another in silence, each contemplating the implications. There was a storm brewing, and John Sullivan might be right in the middle of it.

"I think she's about twenty-five," I said.

"Yes, I think so, too. How old is he?" She said, then took a sip of her Frappuccino.

"He's over sixty. Robbing the cradle, *sí*?" I shuddered.

She sighed, shaking her head.

"Well ... this can't end well. And what if she gets pregnant? Then what?"

I blinked in disbelief. "Pregnant with *him*?"

She shrugged, taking a drink while looking at me.

I fell way back into my chair.

This hadn't come to mind at all.

We stared at one another, the air heavy between us, each thinking of what would happen if *that* happened. I shifted, uncomfortable in my own skin, feeling a shadowy premonition lurking in the days coming our way.

Adele's eyes held a warning. "The man's in dangerous territory, Carli. If what's being said on the streets is true, then it's more than an affair, more than a possible pregnancy. He, himself, might be involved with the cartel."

I shook my head at this, "No, apparently her brothers don't know about them. Yet. I'm more worried that if they find out about the affair, they'll kill him." The words left a sour taste in my mouth.

I hesitated, my heart drumming a nervous beat, but then went ahead and told her. "Luna saw him with a different woman in Parque Juárez this morning. They were arguing." I nodded my head, as if to confirm the weight of my own words.

Her eyebrows shot up to her hairline.

That man kept right on shocking us all.

CHAPTER 7

S ometimes, in life, we worry about the wrong thing. And that's what happened to me.

Here I was thinking that John Sullivan would become a victim of the *Cartel Brothers*, and instead, this happened.

Antonio was too busy or didn't want to tell me anything. And I knew Manuel wouldn't tell me something this gruesome. Besides, perhaps Antonio couldn't share anything about something like even with him, until it was all over.

No. I had to find out in a phone call from, of all people, my head seamstress who lived in the same *colonia* as them. Neighborhood.

She'd called me early this morning, unusual for her. You know how sometimes, before you even answer the phone, you just know that the person on the other end, whoever they might be, has only bad news for you? That's how this was.

My hands shook a little as I took my phone from my night table and looked at the display.

"Hola Josefina, *¿Cómo le va?"* How are you.

I held my breath.

"Oh, Carli, *ni siquiera puedo creerlo."* I can't even believe it.

My heart raced.

"¿Qué quieres decir? ¿Qué no crees?" What do you mean. What don't you believe.

Because she knew about John Sullivan dating *La Señorita*, she thought I'd want to know about this. She'd been shaken by it happening in her own *colonia*, just two streets away from where she lived with her family.

She went on to tell me that, last night, not long after I'd gone to sleep in my home, Dap purring next to me, the oldest Cardero brother, the *sicario,* was found dead on the street in front of his family home, one gunshot to the head and two to the heart—which indicated a professional hit.

The news chilled me. Why would they kill one of their own assassins? He had to have really angered the wrong people. Perhaps he hadn't followed an order, perhaps he'd over-reached. Who knew?

Not long after, when I'd barely managed to get my head around what Josefina had told me, Manuel called. He'd be here later for brunch on the rooftop, so I imagined that he must be calling about what had happened to one of the *Cartel* Brothers. Maybe I should ignore his call. He'd probably just give me a lecture. But, this was Manuel ... so I answered.

"Hola, *primo."* I said, pretending to myself that this was just another, normal, social call from him. He quickly set me straight on that.

"Carlita, listen to me." No "hello cousin" this time. His voice held urgency. He paused, breathing heavy. "I'm telling you right now. This isn't just solving the murder of someone you happen to know."

Somehow, he already knew that I knew about the brother getting gunned down.

He took another deep, audible breath. I could practically hear him gripping the phone. "These people are *dangerous*. They won't hesitate to eliminate *you* if you meddle in their business." He'd never been this stern with me before, not even during that whole other thing. "*¿Lo entiendes*, Carlita? *¿Lo entiendes?*" Do you understand.

I rolled my eyes. "Manuel. You insult me! I'm not *stupida*. No way am I going to have anything to do with no cartel! Do *you* understand?"

My hands shook, and I could hear my own speeding breath, while my heart thumped away. The thing is that I really meant it. There was no way, *no way*, I would get myself involved in solving this one. Right?

But why did he sound so panicked? Did he know something he wasn't telling me? The thought sent my mind racing.

Plus, I didn't *care* about the member of a cartel. I didn't know him, and truly didn't care who shot him or why. It didn't affect anyone in my tribe. John Sullivan surely didn't have anything to do with this either just because he was dating one of the victim's sisters.

I cared about what he did and what happened to John in relation to what he was doing to so many women, but that was it. It was peripheral because he was the husband of one of my customers and that woman, and him, too, socialized with people I cared about, the members of Música Clásica Esencial, an organization important to my mother.

Tension buzzed on the line between us. We finally said terse goodbyes and I hung up, the weight of his warning settling into my bones.

What an incredible mess this was all becoming ...

CHAPTER 8

T hings were a bit chilly between Manuel and me when he first arrived to have Sunday brunch with me on my rooftop, but I did all I could to normalize things between us again. He would"t have it.

"That's it? A renowned chef comes to my house for breakfast, and he brings me a frittata from his competition?"

At least I was making him a cup of his favorite coffee, Blue Jamaican, and it smelled delicious, warm and honeyed.

"Carli, *chica*, don't bust my chops. I worked 'til after midnight. Things were crazy last night. Almost too much business." He began to take the food out of the containers and the scent of frittatas joined the smell of coffee, making my mouth water.

"Oh, *lo siento*—I'm sorry, poor baby," I said, the touch of sarcasm in my voice palpable, "too much business has you down?" I grinned, my eyes twinkling mischievously. But it didn't take.

"Ha ha, Carlita. You're not in my shoes, *mi amor*, don't." He gave me a look that told me he hadn't forgotten our earlier conversation.

As we continued talking, we made our way to the dining table on my rooftop deck. We each put down the trays we were carrying, his with the food plates, mine with a carafe of his coffee and one with matcha tea.

We talked about everyday things, each avoiding what we'd said earlier, which still hovered between us like a bad vibe. Mostly, we ate, he drank his coffee, me my tea, and enjoyed the view.

Then, he shocked me. "I know that family." He said, breaking our silence, like a pebble breaking the water's surface.

"What family?" I lifted my eyes to his, confused.

He looked at me, mouth pursed, eyebrows raised, eyes widened.

"What?" I asked, still confused.

I'd had my mind on this moment here with Manuel, spending time with him alone, the sun warm on my skin, something I cherished, not on the mayhem brewing all around us.

"The Cordero family?" He asked.

Who were they? Why bring them up to me? Then, I realized. "Oh, wait. *La Señorita's* family? That's their name? Antonio wouldn't say."

Dap chose this moment to rise from his sunny spot and to twirl himself around our legs, meowing, his soft fur tickling my ankles. He must have smelled the smoked salmon in the frittata. I took a few small pieces from mine and put them on the ground for him.

"I know, but you'll find out soon, enough, Yes, them." Said Manuel, ignoring Dap, intent on what he wanted to tell me.

"Okay, I'm curious, go ahead."

"Go ahead? What are you, a princess giving me permission to speak?"

"No, your queen!" I laughed.

He ignored my attempt at humor and continued. My heart sank at his rebuff.

"I dated her older sister for a few months, back in my *policia* days." He said it in that tone of voice we all use when we don't really want to tell someone something.

I sat up straight at this, feeling a sudden rush of adrenaline.

"What?! You dated the sister of *cartel* guys while you were a cop? Manuel!"

"They weren't at the time!" He exclaimed, putting both hands up like stop signs, eyes wide. "Though, I have to say, I saw signs. They were just starting their careers was my guess."

He sighed, the weight of the memory heavy in his voice. "It's one reason I broke it off." He shrugged as if trying to get comfortable in his skin.

I collapsed back into the cushions of my chair, the soft fabric enveloping me like a cocoon.

"Oh. What were they like? The whole family, I mean."

"Not well off at the time, struggling, like many here, as you know."

I nodded, taking in the sounds that floated up from the neighborhood below. San Miguel, like the rest of Mexico, had its haves and have-nots. The well-off enjoyed life, while the poor dreamt of a better life. A rising middle class was disrupting the status quo, but the odds remained uneven. Some, feeling stuck, opted for shortcuts, seeing cartels as a quick path to wealth. No education or experience needed—just the guts to commit heinous acts on the *jefe*'s orders. The Boss.

"What signs? You said you saw signs."

"Well, the struggle, their simmering anger, odd people coming and going—I felt it all when I'd pick up Eliana. How they held back in conversation with me. What I saw put me off, so I broke things off with her when she said she was moving to Guadalajara for a new job." He stopped to take a sip of his coffee.

"All I needed was them trying something with me when I was thinking of leaving the force." He gazed pensively into the distance while he spoke, as if he were in a trance.

My eyes drilled right into the heart of him. But my own heart took a break from beating for a beat or so, its absence echoing in my ears. He'd never said.

With the *cartel* growing increasingly hostile toward police—especially in Guanajuato, just a short drive away—why keep his family in the dark? We could have kept an eye out, made sure no one watched him, followed him? Send him into hiding for a bit?

Of *course* he'd thought of it. Of course. But, being first, somewhat *macho*, then Mexican, then Manuel, he'd never have named this as one of the reasons for quitting the force, going to culinary school, and opening his restaurant. The unsaid hung heavy between us, like a thick fog.

His dream hadn't come true due to pure will. A life-threatening situation had fueled it. Would the dream have ever taken off without that danger lurking around him?

I stared at him until his eyebrows moved up to nearly his hairline and he put out his jaw in defiance, a hint of challenge in his gaze. I blinked out of a reverie of him getting gunned down by thugs.

I cleared my throat, the sound raspy against what had become once again a tense atmosphere.

Dap, who'd returned to lie in his favorite sunny spot, now came back to us and plopped himself down at my feet. And meowed, the sound breaking through the tension, though we both ignored him.

"What's her younger sister's name? The one seeing John Sullivan?" I asked, pushing away my empty plate.

"Camila." He took another sip of coffee and set the cup back down.

"How come you didn't tell me about dating her sister?" I more or less mumbled. He usually told me who he was dating. It often felt as if he did it so I'd find out from him and not someone else. As if he felt guilty for dating someone else.

"You were in New York," he uttered, glancing toward the Parroquia. And as if he'd called for it, its bells went off, calling parishioners and visitors to mass.

We waited for the tolling to stop. His gaze returned to the table, where he deliberately rearranged his used silverware on his plate, the clinking sound rhythmic and soothing.

"Knowing what you know about them, do you think they'll interfere in their sister's affair with John Sullivan?"

He shifted his gaze from the table to me, the intensity of his stare like a spotlight, and almost as if he'd just noticed my presence. Disbelief at my question ran rampant on his face. He faced me squarely, looking prepared to enlighten me, rather than berate what he considered my eternal optimism about people.

He stood. "Carlita, dudes like that can't let something like this slip. They'd look weak in front of their guys, and they can't afford that. I have to go." He put our plates and cutlery and napkins onto a tray and faced me.

"Like I said before, *stay out of it*!"

The intensity of his gaze scorched me where I sat. I felt glued to my chair, while without giving me another look headed to the staircase. Quickly, I gathered the French presses and cups and condiments and followed him.

My heart raced. I didn't want him to leave while we were at odds, but it seemed impossible. He feared for my life.

Once we'd put everything away in the kitchen, he left. But not before opening his arms wide to me and taking me into his embrace. I nearly cried. Even though he was angry with me, he still loved me.

After he left, I got ready for a massage appointment at my friend's spa. To change my mood, I slipped into Anjali Luna harem pants in ocean, paired them with a black Lululemon jacket, and slipped on black Coach sneakers. Maybe I'd invite Ana to a late *comida*.

I filled Dap's water and dry food bowls, scratched him around the ears a little so he'd hopefully forgive me for leaving him, and left out the door.

The moment I stepped into Ana's spa, I sensed that today's visit would be different, as if trouble traveled in the very air.

CHAPTER 9

When I entered, things seemed normal enough. I breathed in the warm, relaxing scent of her propriety blend of essential oils always diffusing during opening hours. Notes of lavender and lemon verbena permeated the air, but with undertones of other, difficult-to-detect scents, and she wouldn't share her recipe.

Sarah Brightman's ethereal tones floated through the air, making the space feel even more inviting. I could live here!

From the check-in counter, her voice melded with the ambiance. "Hola Carli, *bienvenido, amiga!*"

I replied with a cheerful, "*Hola*, Ana!"

Her faint jasmine perfume enveloped me when I leaned to kiss her cheek. "Ready for some deep relaxation?" Her soft, chocolate-brown eyes met mine, gauging my needs for the session.

"Never been more ready!" I exclaimed, while I couldn't help but notice a deeper unease gripping my friend—like the invisible undertow of the ocean. Was something dragging her down? Could I help?

"Ana, want to have a late *comida* with me after?" I asked, hopeful. "I have to go to my shop for a few minutes when I leave here, but we could meet somewhere after."

She hesitated, tucking a strand of hair behind her ear. "Oh, Carli ... I'd love to, but I have John and Lisa after you," she said, a note of apology in her voice, as she adjusted a stack of fresh towels on the counter.

I knew the "couple of the hour" were among the select few clients Ana still personally attended to.

"Ah well, maybe another time, *sí*?"

"Por supuesto!" Of course. Her eyes met mine briefly before looking away again.

"Want to make plans for this week?"

She weighed her response, as if on the fulcrum of a teeter-tot-ter, not knowing which way to fall, while her hand hovered over the towels.

"Sí, sure. I'll text?"

This indecisiveness didn't sound like the Ana I knew. It made me uneasy.

"Alright," I murmured, the weight of uncertainty deepening.

She straightened up, clearly ready to move on. "Well, ready?" She led the way down the corridor to a massage room.

After a sublime massage, I hugged Ana goodbye, reminding her to text me when she could meet for *comida*, or even dinner.

I headed home, and to calm myself and take my mind off of things, I sketched, erased, redrew, tearing up one sheet after another, a vision I'd had finally transferring to paper.

As I reached out to put my sketch pad back on the table, I realized my silver cuff bracelet—with its three emerald stones, one for each decade of my life—was missing. A memory of it resting on Ana's massage room counter flashed. My 30th birthday gift from Manuel, its sentimental value made leaving it there overnight unthinkable.

Dialing Ana, I hit voicemail, and quickly asked her to wait for my return. Upon reaching Ana's, I spotted her behind the counter, her gaze distant. I tapped softly on the glass door. She jolted upright, staring briefly as if not recognizing me. Though she quickly composed herself as she came to the door, my intuition sensed her turmoil.

"Carli, *hola*, come in. I have it in the drawer." She returned behind the counter, and retrieved my beloved bracelet, which I slipped onto my arm. How could I not have noticed it hadn't been there for all those hours?

But Fate knows why she does what she does. In this case, sending me back to Ana's after John and Lisa had left.

And just then—because I'd had the feeling before—I realized Lisa was about to add to the sea of complications around me.

CHAPTER 10

A na looked more troubled than before.

"Todo bien, Ana?" I asked, concern tinging my voice.

"Sí, sí, Carli, *está bien*," she brushed me off, but her demeanor screamed otherwise.

"Let's grab coffee or maybe an early dinner? You seem off," I pushed gently.

After a sigh and a distant gaze, she relented, "Alright, Carli. You win. Let's go eat."

We chuckled lightly, a moment of levity.

Walking beneath the bluest of skies, contrasting her mood, which affected mine, we settled at a tucked-away table in a bistro. A server uncorked a bottle of rosé, which lightened the atmosphere a bit, and we ordered roast chicken and veggies.

Raising my glass, I offered, "Let's toast to the best life we can have."

She didn't lift her own glass. Her eyes searched mine as if looking for an answer as to what that might be for her.

"Okay, but really, I'm not sure that will happen for me anymore."

She hesitated, and my heart sank. I felt her anguish, as if the blanket of a humid day pressed down on her whole life. Surely, things couldn't be so bad for my beautiful, usually happy, friend?

"Oh, Ana ..." I paused, unable to think of what to say to that.

"Well, then you tell me what's going on, and we fix it. Together, *sí*?"

Giving her my biggest encouraging smile, I lifted my glass in encouragement for her to do the same.

With a small smile, she finally picked up her own glass and clinked it with mine. The tinkling sound brought some joy back to our space.

"To our best life yet!" I toasted. She repeated after me. We each took a small sip and put our glasses back down.

"So, tell me." I opened my arms wide, hands flat, giving her the floor, so to speak.

She opened her mouth to speak, but just then, music came on at a volume unacceptable for conversation. I gestured to our server to turn it down. She nodded, mouthing "*lo siento*," and took off toward the back. Soon, the volume lowered to something more reasonable.

I raised my eyebrows at Ana and lifted my chin in her direction at the same time.

As if resigned, she finally opened up.

"Carli, first you have to promise to not tell anyone this, *sí? Manténgase a sí mismo.*"

"Of course, I keep it to myself." I toyed with the stem of my wine glass.

"Thank you." She smiled at me, but not her usual, the one of a person at peace. Sad, more like it.

I felt a pinch in my heart.

She hesitated once more, took a not-lady-like gulp of wine, and her eyes probing mine, said just two words.

"John. Sullivan."

This confused me. What could one of her massage clients have to do with her distraught mood? Then, it came to me. Oh, no. Oh, no ... not Ana, too?

She'd clearly followed the reasoning playing out on my face. Her eyes still on mine, she simply nodded.

"Why?" I asked. Stupid question, duh.

Why did women repeatedly trust deceivers, despite having evolved to be wiser? Was it a deep-rooted belief in humanity's goodness or a primal drive in our DNA, compelling us to believe lies just to ensure the species' survival?

Someone dropped a plate onto the tile floor in the back of the restaurant. Its resonant clatter as it shattered startled us, though we didn't turn our heads that way, a testament to the stress her admission caused us both.

Ana shrugged.

I waited her out. Best let her explain.

"I fell for the story they all say." She shook her head back and forth, her mouth puckered in disappointment at herself. "That he was leaving her. He said we would build our lives together."

I felt transfixed, my eyes glued to hers as if by opposite magnets. Her face bright red now. Should I say something about *La Señorita*? Did Ana know?

She took another sip of wine, and I did, too. One needed reinforcement to deal with such a revelation.

Her demeanor shifted abruptly. Anger blazed in her eyes. She grasped her wine glass, taking a hefty gulp as if parched from a journey in the desert. Or, as if bracing for battle.

"He said they've been unhappy for years, that they don't even sleep in the same room anymore. That he wanted me instead. That he loved me. And then ... then, I found out ..."

I held my breath. She knew ...

Suddenly, she straightened, her posture royal and dignified.

"During his massage today, I wanted to strangle him! *Pendejo*!" Idiot. "I can't believe he had the nerve to come for a massage after telling me he was breaking off things." Tears formed in her eyes.

I froze.

"Oh, Ana."

"I should have used peanut oil for his massage," she muttered, no oomph in it, her gaze fixed on the table. What? Why? Wait ... "Ana, is John allergic?" My whole being went on alert.

She nodded.

"But you didn't use that, right?" I held my breath.

She shook her head no, looking at her wine glass in her hand, not at me. The woman was angry. I'd never seen Ana this way. Never.

I tried to comfort her, but she pulled away, then our food arrived.

"So, the massages started it all?" I probed.

"No, it began at Central Market, in the wine aisle. He asked me out for coffee," she confessed, her cheeks burning with shame. "He lamented about Lisa, claiming he was nearly done with her. But every Sunday, they'd show up together. And when Lisa would pop over to El Café during his session, we'd ..." she trailed off.

I nodded, sympathetically. The tale was tragic, and evidently, hadn't reached "The End" yet.

"So, today, I acted professionally, not even allowing him to touch my legs or arms, nodding toward the reception the two times he tried. When I was done, I walked out of the room before he could say anything."

"And then ..." Ana's eyes glistened with tears.

"He ... he'd been seeing someone else. Not just me, Carli." Her hand tightened on the stem of her wine glass and her whole stance changed, her body as rigid as a statue of herself. Rage emanated from her, forming a wall behind which fury sent daggers from her eyes into something only she could see.

Ah, she knew. A deep breath slowly left my body as if I'd been holding it since she'd started her tale. Still, such anger, especially coming from her, unsettled me.

"Oh, Ana. I'm so, so, sorry, *querida*." Dear.

"She's just a girl. A girl, Carli!" She exclaimed; her tears now fell, creating twin waterfalls on her cheeks.

"I know, Ana, so sorry."

She seemed to come out of her trance, then. "You know? You *knew*?" She sniffed, grabbed a tissue from her handbag and patted her eyes.

The lights went down a bit in the restaurant, the music changed to slower beats, creating a more romantic atmosphere for evening diners. I looked around for the first time since we'd arrived, and saw that people now occupied at least half the tables. And a party of four waited by the hostess stand with more people just coming in the door behind them.

"Did everyone?" She asked, then, her eyebrows raised at me in question. She blushed deeply.

"Well, not everyone, I don't think, but a few people. What surprises me more is you. I didn't know about your af ... well, about you and him," I ended lamely.

She huffed.

"How did you find out? About her, the girl, I mean." I asked her.

"I went to Los Mezquites on Thursday afternoon to visit my sister. When I turned the corner onto her street, there he was, just ahead of me, walking hand in hand with ...," she gulped, "that ... that *child*."

Ana's grip tightened on her wine glass and table's edge. I feared her despair might push her to extremes, like scorned women throughout history who'd killed their lover or husband over another woman.

"He didn't see you." I said, rhetorically.

"No ... I," she sighed deeply before continuing. "Without thinking, I turned around and went back the way I'd come, around the corner. My sister lives nearby. I didn't want to cause her embarrassment." She shook her head, frustrated with herself. "Like an *idiota*, I stood there, on the sidewalk, my heart pounding, my whole body shaking. Like I should be the one ashamed instead of him!"

"Oh, Ana." My heart grieved for her.

"I should have faced him, Carli. I can't explain why I didn't."

Our eyes locked for a moment. Thank goodness she hadn't.

"Look, Ana. Do you know about the girl's brothers?"

She didn't answer right away. Then, she nodded her head. Took up her wine glass and sipped on it, looking down at the table. Then, got teary again.

"I don't know what to do, Carli. I *love* him. Really love him. Of all the stupid things I could do. Fall in love with a married man. Who cheats on his wife. With me. And with another woman too!" She took a sip of wine and put her glass back down on the table. I waited.

"He called me later that day, and asked me to meet him in Parque Juárez." She huffed. "He said that he couldn't see me anymore, that he was staying in his marriage."

So, this is who Luna had seen arguing with John in the park. She'd never met Ana, so didn't know her by sight.

Ana shuddered. I took her hand in mine once more. This time, she let me keep it, limp as it was.

How had Lisa not figured it out? Ana, and *La Señorita*—Camila. She had a face, a name, and I should use it. One man's bad behavior shouldn't be blamed on a barely twenty-two-year-old girl. And sure, John and Lisa busied themselves with their different interests, but in a small city like San Miguel there was only so much cheating one could hide.

Only one answer to that. Lisa knew. And for some reason, she chose to ignore it. Why?

Ana suddenly seemed disoriented, glancing around the restaurant before her eyes met mine, heavy with the weight of her confessions. She leaned in, her nearly untouched meal pushed aside

"Carli, forget what I've said," she whispered, eyes darting suspiciously. "About the peanut oil. I need to distance myself from him. You believe I'd never harm him, right?"

Her eyes pleaded for my trust. I wrestled with doubt—thinking of the adage about a woman scorned. This man's deceit wronged a woman I held dear. How many others had he toyed with? My heart ached for Ana.

I wanted to believe her, I really did, but, you know, a woman scorned and all that.

How dare he use these women in this way? In *my* town. *My* friend. And a young girl who hadn't yet learned to know better. Who else had he done this to? Poor Ana!

We finally finished our very late *comida*. The server looked relieved when we asked for the check, what with several people now waiting for tables.

Just as he left our table with my credit card, my phone buzzed. I opened the flap of my handbag to just look at my phone and who was calling. Antonio. With everything going on, I wanted to take his call.

"Do you mind? It's Antonio. I'll just say I'll call him later."

Ana just waived at me to answer.

"Hola Antonio. *¿Cómo estás, primo?"*

"Hola chica. You're going to make Manuel jealous by calling me *primo."*

I rolled my eyes. "You called to tell me that?"

He chuckled. "No, I thought you might want to know that John Sullivan was brought to Hospital MAC."

My heart nearly stopped. I stared at Ana.

But, first, what about the cartel brother with bullets in his head and heart?

Urgently, I asked. "Antonio, what about the brother? Camila's brother? Josefina said that he's been ..."

He interrupted me.

"I'm not discussing that with you at all. Not now. Not ever." I heard him take a deep breath. "So, don't ask, okay?"

Well, no, not really okay, but what could I do? I pivoted back to John Sullivan because ... wait. Had he said that he saw John at the hospital? I'd been so focused on finding out about the brothers that my brain had ignored that. I gripped my phone to the point where my knuckles hurt.

"What ... what do you mean John's in the hospital? How do you know?"

My body shot straight up in my chair of its own accord; a rubber band stretched tight.

"I was here to visit the father of one of my detectives. He always feeds us *comida*, you know, and now he's had a heart attack. He's doing well, but I came to pay my respects anyway. I didn't have much time because I'm dealing with that murder now."

"So? John? What happened to him?" I asked, worrying my bottom lip.

"Oh. I was just leaving through the Emergency Room doors, and they were bringing him in on a gurney."

Chapter 11

Antonio's pronouncement left me speechless. The sounds of the restaurant faded into the background. The moment felt surreal. Ana had just told me of different ways she could have killed John, and now he'd been taken to a hospital. On a stretcher.

"Carli, hello?" Asked Antonio, his voice piercing through hazy fog in my head.

"You alright?" He added, concern evident in his tone.

My breathing shallow, all I could do was stare at Ana. Who returned the favor, her hands now fisted, her knuckles white. No doubt she felt my conversation with Antonio somehow affected her.

Finally, she asked, loudly, "*¿Mande?*" What. The clatter of cutlery stopped momentarily, making her voice sound even louder, which caused people at the tables closest to us to look our way. Ana blushed, her cheeks now painted a deep shade of red, realizing she'd invited unwanted attention.

"Antonio? I have to go. I'm at *comida* with Ana. We're just leaving. Can I call you back once I'm home?"

"Oh, *there* you are." He asked, fake-irritated. "*Sí, no problemo*, call me later. *Ciao*." He hung up, the finality of the call echoing in my ears.

Ana asked again, this time in a whisper filled with anxiety, "*¿Mande* Carli?" as the server brought back my credit card and the slip for me to sign.

I put up a finger in the universal wait-a-minute sign, added a tip to the credit card slip, did up the total, signed and that was that. Now I could answer Ana and focus on her reaction.

"That was Antonio."

She nodded, her brow furrowing, her eyelashes casting shadows on her high cheekbones, and I realized she already knew that.

"He said he was at Hospital MAC and saw John being brought in on a stretcher."

Ana slapped a hand over her mouth like one trying to keep in a scream. Genuine reaction, as far as I could tell. But the real anger in her eyes when she told me about John cheating on her with Camila of the Cartel Brothers (here I went, another nickname for *La Señorita*) came back to me, hazy, something I didn't want to see, yet ...

"What happened? Oh my God, Carli, what happened?"

She stood, her chair scraping against the floor, and I could tell she had in mind to go over there.

"No, Ana. No!"

She sat back down, gingerly, as if she'd never been introduced to a chair before, feeling one for the first time, the plush cushion yielding under her weight.

"You can't go over there. Not now. It would only make sense if Lisa asked you to."

We both knew that Lisa wouldn't have a reason to ask their massage therapist to visit her husband in the hospital.

What if he didn't make it? Why was he there? Seemed that if Manuel knew, he'd have told me. Right? Maybe not with his attitude lately, pfft. I'd have to wait to know until I got home and called Antonio.

"Well, what happened? What did Antonio say?"

If this was a performance to cover something she'd done to John this afternoon, she deserved an Emmy. No, an Oscar. Both!

"Didn't ask. I'm calling him as soon as I get home. I'll let you know. Let's go. People are starting to look our way more and more."

She gazed around the restaurant and stood, the soft rustling of her dress filling the brief silence. She grabbed her handbag, and led the way outside.

We headed toward El Jardin, mostly silent.

From here, Ana went one way to her home, and I went the other to mine. We hugged goodbye before we separated. Clouds filled her eyes, shimmering with unshed tears.

Had I just hugged a murderess?

Why did these things always happen to me? Other people's problems? Murders? I'd moved back to San Miguel for a simpler life without mayhem!

I shook my head, walking slowly toward home, the rhythmic patter of my footsteps echoing my contemplation, while I tried to puzzle out the whole John Sullivan thing.

Those brothers of Camila's? Wouldn't they normally have wanted to get rid of John? But being so busy with their brother's murder, and the fact that the brother who'd been killed was the *sicario* in the family ... perhaps any vendetta against John would be put on hold?

Then, there was Ana. All that rage. Never, ever, had I seen that in her before. Her dark side.

And, Lisa couldn't be discounted. She *must* know. She must. How could he go around cheating that much and the person he lived with not realize it? If so, what was it? Did they have an arrangement? Or did Lisa have a reason to keep silent? Did she have plans of her own to put a stop to it all? To put a stop to *him*?

A heaviness settled in my chest.

I got home, finally, the familiar scent of my living room giving a moment of relief. I found Dap just inside my door, which, of course, meant he probably felt my distress. I grabbed him up, his warm, furry body immediately grounding me.

Without so much as going to my closet to drop off my handbag and slip out of my shoes, I flopped on the couch, Dap in my arms like a baby. And he let me hold him like that. Which proved he felt my anguish.

Should I call Antonio back now? The weight of the phone in my hand felt almost too heavy to lift.

I mean, what if what he told me pointed to Ana having poisoned John?

Was he at the hospital because he'd gone into a terrifying spiral of anaphylaxis shock from having been exposed to peanut oil?

CHAPTER 12

The next morning, I dashed to my Allende workshop, where the magic of my designs came together. I spent every Monday and Thursday mornings there. Even with mayhem all around me.

But Monday evenings? Those were reserved for what I called *Culling of the Clothes*. This meant scouring the clothing racks, often way past sunset, ensuring only the freshest and most vibrant threads remained.

Today, I'd made a huge effort to carry out the culling throughout the day instead. Because, this evening, Manuel and I aimed to go La Taberna Clandestina's for live piano music. He still wanted to go.

We were trying to have a normal life despite all the turmoil around us. Well, okay, it was me trying to do that. Manuel was staying completely out of the investigation, so his life was proceeding as usual.

I walked to Manuel's Eatery where we'd agreed to meet, the life of Centro buzzing around me. My heels clicked against the cobblestones, punctuating my thoughts as my mind drifted to my conversation with Antonio the night before—the one after I got home.

As expected, Antonio had strongly cautioned me away from John Sullivan and Lisa Martin for now.

"Why?" I'd asked. Of course, with the brother of one of John's mistresses having gotten killed and who knew who was next, he had a point.

"Carli, I can't always tell you everything, you know that." He said to me, his favorite cousin (in my own mind, anyway).

Ah! I could still feel the tension that had crackled between us like dry twigs underfoot in a silent forest. He hated that I had solved crimes ahead of him, something he felt should be left to himself, the *Sargento de Investigación* (detective sergeant), to his boss, the prosecutor, and to the detectives he supervised. But with the police force here being overwhelmed, as everywhere in Mexico, surely he was grateful for my involvement?

¿Sí? ¿No? I chuckled at that. At the same time, I knew he hated to see me put myself in danger. When that happened, he'd berate me for weeks about what he called my "irresponsible behavior." He'd been so angry with me for so long when I'd solved a different murder, just six months ago.

I understood about giving the *cartel* brother murder a wide berth. But how could I heed his caution about John and Lisa?

"But ... you want me to stay away from people I run into all the time, Antonio ..." I whined.

He groaned, a sound like that of an old door creaking open.

"We're hearing rumors, Carli. About that Camila. Well, her remaining brothers to be more specific."

"Oh. What kind of rumors?" My heart beat against my chest in a fast rhythm. Would another brother be killed? Or would they kill someone? "They're not taking kindly to a *gringo* messing with their sister. Even now. A *married gringo*. An *old* married gringo. We heard it on the streets. When I saw him come in on a stretcher, for a minute, I almost assumed that they must have had something to do with it."

"And?" I held my breath for his response.

"Nada."

"What do you mean, nothing?"

"Wasn't them. Apparently, among other medical problems, John is allergic to peanuts, and ..."

I dropped my phone. Or it slipped from my hands. I don't know. But it fell and seemed to disappear into the mess of a velvety textured throw and Dap next to me on the couch. I finally got it back after a frantic search conducted with both hands. Dap meowed loudly and jumped off the couch when I moved him aside, shooting me his best are-you-kidding-me look, a displeased monarch dethroned from his perch.

"WHAT? Antonio?" No one could miss the anxiety in my voice.

"Carli? *What*, what?" Asked a confused Antonio.

"I dropped my phone. I didn't hear what you said."

Ana had done it! She'd used peanut oil on John. *She'd lied to me!* But surely that wouldn't *kill* him? Or cause that big of an allergic reaction? Didn't people with a peanut allergy have to ingest them to react?

"Oh. I said Sullivan ate at a restaurant where they used peanut oil."

My whole body collapsed inwardly in relief. It wasn't Ana's fault.

Calm washed over me like cool water on a sweltering day, nearly making me drop the phone again. My hands began to shake. My fingers trembled, and I fell back into my beautiful down-filled Henredon couch (snapped from a consignor, of course, about two years back), so relieved for Ana.

"Wait. Is he okay? I heard he's allergic."

"*Sí*. The restaurant, whose owner happens to be allergic to peanuts, too, keeps EpiPens on hand, so a waiter grabbed one when he realized what was happening, and injected Sullivan with it."

"*Ay*, wow, such drama!"

"Now, of course, the restaurant swears they don't use peanut oil in the cooking, just peanuts in some dishes. They claim they don't use peanuts in the chicken tamales which is what he ate, or peanut oil to cook them, or anything in. So, as of now, it's a mystery how he got peanuts, or oil, in him."

"Why the hospital?"

"Ah, a busboy called for an ambulance first thing, and since Sullivan still looked dazed and they worried something else might be going on, they decided to take him to the hospital. And, that's where we 'met'." As if him seeing John on a stretcher in the emergency room had been an arranged meeting. He laughed.

"That's not funny."

His sigh was long and weary, threading through the phone line.

"I have to see the humor where I can, *chica.* You know. And anyway, he's okay, they released him to go home after a couple hours."

My insides had untwisted somewhat but not entirely. At least, I'd remembered to breathe again. No trouble for Ana. But John and Lisa should be avoided, by me—by everyone—for a while, until his affair with *Camila of the Cartel Brothers* got sorted out.

First, a dead cartel brother. Second, an apparently poisoned John? Had it been a mistake or deliberate? Could it still be Ana and it just took a while for peanut oil to work itself in when it was used on the body?

My unsettled feeling made a comeback, stronger and more insistent, like the distant rumble of an approaching storm increasing in intensity.

Chapter 13

B y the time work had ended, I'd reconsidered my outfit plans for the evening with Manuel. My eyes were set on that vintage Emilio Pucci jumpsuit tucked away in my home closet, a must for the Sinatra-themed night at La Taberna Clandestina. The swirl of electrifying colors—apple green, teal, beige, black, sky blue—melded into a dance of ovals, squares, and triangles. Listening to that music and wearing this outfit would be like a Mia Farrow moment watching Sinatra with an impatient heart at The Dunes in Las Vegas.

So, as soon as I got home, I headed to the jewel of my house: the perfect closet I'd had built an adjoining bedroom. A cousin electrician had it illuminated perfectly. It boasted glass-front drawers and a triple mirror dominated a corner.

I paired the jumpsuit with off-white Courrèges go-go boots, a nod to the original creator before the world made copies. These boots, tailored with a soft lining and perfect heel height, made cobblestone streets a walk in the park. They were perfect for the evening's journey, which included a brief walk to Manuel's Eatery on Umaran, a longer stride to the bar on Mesones, and finally, the route home on Privada Pila Seca.

Before heading out, I bribed Dap with his favorite treats and a splash of milk. His skeptical eyes followed me, clutching a treat between his teeth, as he vanished under the couch.

Ready to go in my retro ensemble, I felt a surge of joy. The evening promised to be fun, and I wouldn't let the John Sullivan and a little ol' *cartel* murder shambles get in the way of a great evening with Manuel. Wishing there could be more, as usual.

I headed out the door once more, and couldn't keep the recent events from dancing in my head. Lisa puzzled me. How could she not know about all these affairs? I wondered for the millionth time. Might she plan to do something about it? Or did she simply plan to ignore it for the sake of staying in the marriage? Not everyone thought cheating was the end of the world. Could it be she simply didn't care?

When I entered the restaurant, I said hello to the hostess and noticed that the place was packed, so I told her I'd wait for Manuel in his office. Though Manuel would argue with me to sit at one of two empty barstools and have a glass of wine, no way did I want to interfere with even just a few more *pesos* making it into his register. Without being seated right away, people could just leave rather than wait.

On my way toward the back, the sight of John and Lisa in one of the semi-private booths shocked me. The warm amber glow from the chandelier above their table made it even more surreal. He'd been at the hospital just yesterday. Now, here he was, dining out? I turned my head the other way quickly, hoping they wouldn't see me. But they were deeply engrossed in a conversation, and I slipped right past them, the soft murmur of other diners covering the sound of my footsteps.

I closed the office door, feeling as if I'd escaped being caught at something forbidden. I sat in Manuel's vintage chair, and the scent of old leather teased my nostrils. I chuckled at my own silliness.

It's when I heard John's voice, faint, and noticeably stressed, that I recalled the booth in which they sat had a strange acoustical element almost no one knew about. Despite the faint hum of the AC above, a conversation going on in that booth could be heard here in Manuel's office, though somewhat muffled. Still, one could make out words if one focused.

No one could figure the why or how of this phenomenon, so nothing had been done about it. Something to do with the venting system, but the expense of changing it would cost too much. Plus, Manuel mainly worked in here when there were few patrons in the house, and the hostess knew to only seat people there if all other semi-private rooms were occupied and the customers insisted on one.

Normally, I'd go into Manuel's computer and log onto Spotify to hear music instead of them, but with all the goings-on with these two lately, curiosity got the better of me.

The shock I got for doing so made me wish I could rewind back a few minutes.

"But, no, John, no, we're not doing that." Lisa sounded plaintive, her voice quivering like a violin string, sounding like a small child who'd been refused her favorite toy.

What had he said to her?

"Yes, Lisa. It's time. We're not happy ... you *know* that ..." John. He sounded plaintive himself.

Was he asking for what I thought he was asking her? I placed my hand over my mouth in shock, taking in a short, stressed breath.

Silence. Then, the distinct clink of silverware hitting porcelain.

"I don't want a divorce. I'm not giving you one." Lisa, affirmative, sounding sure of herself suddenly.

I held my breath, the weight of the moment pressing down, my eyes on the door as if they were right there on the other side, instead of in a booth halfway to the entrance. "Lisa ..."

"No, John. No. That's my last word on it, eh."

"Not mine." He sounded aggressive, his words and the energy behind them crackling like live wires.

Lisa sighed so loudly that I heard it.

"Look, I'll help you get a place of your own, here or in Toronto." I heard cutlery clanging against stoneware. No response from her.

"You might be better off in Toronto. With your family being there, I mean, eh." Said the man who most likely wanted her out of his way here in our small town.

He probably didn't want to run into her, a reminder of his cowardliness, of his sins. With Lisa gone, their social circle, sipping on their evening wines and whispering stories, would remember he'd dumped her for that much younger woman. Nevertheless, in time, they'd resume socializing with the one who still lived here. They'd lose touch with Lisa, the memory of her laughter, spirit, and gossipy ways fading over time like an old photograph.

"Why? So you don't have to see me here, John?" The venom-laced words slithered out of her mouth, sharp and piercing like a cold gust of wind.

Well, there you go.

And. Who was he divorcing her for? Ana? No. He broke up with her. *La Señorita?* Maybe she really was pregnant, and he wanted to make one thing right by marrying her?

The silence that followed was suffocating, and the tension hung thick.

CHAPTER 14

The office door opened so suddenly that I jumped up like a guilty someone. That I was. Guilty of eavesdropping on Lisa and John's conversation.

"Carli?" Manuel asked, puzzlement playing on his face. "*¿Está pasando?*" What's going on. "Nothing, uh, I mean ... well ...

"Ah, *todo*, Manuel. *Todo*!" Everything. Everything is wrong.

Manuel, beautiful being that he is, encircled me in his strong arms in a way he'd most likely do frequently were we not forbidden to one another. His tall, buff frame, one worthy of any gym rat, which he wasn't, fit perfectly against my five-foot-seven self. I collapsed against him. Barefoot—as I was now—the top of my head fit on his Adam's apple, and my face rested at the peak of his chest as if custom made for me.

"What, *mi chica*, what happened?"

He spoke softly, as if to a small, scared girl, running a hand over my hair, rocking me gently back and forth.

Then, he kissed my forehead, his lips lingering there much longer than a chaste kiss between cousins called for. My heart began to pound, my insides to melt, my legs to weaken. Arms too. "Oh, *dios mio*!" I whispered. Oh, my goodness. But to stay in his arms forever! Yet, the pull of family tradition was strong in me, in him, too, and so we retreated from one another, the moment awkward. I feared we'd open a Pandora's box we'd be unable to close again.

He wanted me too. I knew this more and more lately, with every stolen glance, with the electric charge in the air when-ever our paths crossed. Our proud family, however, saw it differently. I didn't understand. Studies showed that there were no more birth defects between cousins, definitely not fourth cousins, than for people totally unrelated.

But in addition to that, we knew our parents feared family rifts if cousins married, especially since so many worked in the family enterprises. Manuel and I, however, didn't even work on the hacienda, and most likely never would.

Some say that if you fall in love under the magic of San Miguel, you must leave it with your lover to test the truth of your feelings. My family and Manuel's had vacationed together numerous times: Mexico City, Texas, California, and Spain. We'd been younger, though, the sweet scent of adolescence still on us. The last of such trips took place when we'd both been fourteen years old. I hadn't realized yet that I'd been in love with Manuel, so there'd been no romance to test. Plus, we'd been so young, too young.

While in New York City, however, during the few days our paths had crossed, we'd both felt the air sizzling between us, two high-voltage power lines grazing against one another ...

Strangely, nothing but silence on this matter came from my dead bio-father whom I consulted on all important matters. My little secret. My whole life, I'd felt a closeness to the man who'd fathered me, despite his death having occurred before my birth.

In a favorite snapshot of him with my mother, their eyes sparkled so that they obliterated nearly everything else in the photo, like the sun blasting through a cloud. Though they faced the camera their eyes slanted toward one another's, immense love pouring from one onto the other.

In times of distress, that photo tight in my hands or nearby, I'd speak to him. In my head mostly, but sometimes out loud, as Dap well knew. Then, I'd wait for his answers. My dad's, that is. Which sometimes came, sometimes not.

Now, though I'd pulled back from Manuel as much as possible with his hands still clasped behind my waist. It seemed he couldn't let go. A beat in time. I could survive a whole month by feeding on nothing but this moment alone.

A knock at the door startled both of us. Manuel let go as if extricating himself from a fire. "*¿Mande?*" He called out, having turned toward the door though I felt his energy still bound to mine.

"Manuel, *no es posible servir zanahorias con el salmón esta noche"* Called a voice from the other side. Couldn't serve carrots with the salmon tonight? Then serve something else, I thought. I resented the interruption.

Manuel tsk'd a few times, and opened the door slightly, hiding me from whoever stood there.

"Por qué no?" Why not? He asked, annoyance in every sylla-ble.

"Carlos dice que las zanahorias son demasiado suaves no son buenas." Carlos says the carrots are too soft, they're not good.

"Use los espárragos que obtuvimos para mañana en su lugar." Use the asparagus we got for tomorrow instead.

"Bien, gracias, Manuel." Thank you.

Manuel closed the door and turned to me slowly. Our eyes locked saying more than words could ever convey. Another knock at the door annoyed us, but a smile began to form on Manuel's lips, then on mine, and immediately, we both chuckled. The Universe interfering, most likely at the request of our parents.

"Venida!" I'm coming. He called out, then turned to me. "I'll be back in a minute. Will you be ready to go then?"

I simply nodded my head, and began to listen for John and Lisa again, but heard nothing. Glancing at the security cameras lining the wall next to Manuel's desk, I saw that they'd left.

How had it ended? Had Lisa agreed to a divorce? Had John agreed to not divorce her after all?

Manuel came back in, sat across from the desk, and smiled at me. "*Sí, Señor* Cano, what can I do for you?" I asked, putting on a haughty air.

"Ah! You can tell me what you were so upset about earlier."

I deflated. He hadn't forgotten.

"Well, you know that weird thing with the acoustics?"

He glanced at the vent, and nodded. "What did you hear?" He asked, looking curious.

I took a deep breath and looked him right in the eye.

"John Sullivan asked Lisa Martin for a divorce."

His mouth dropped open. Eyes widening, he stood and turned toward the camera monitors looking for the couple. He brushed a hand through his hair, disrupting its usual order.

"Well ... is he insane? Leaving her for Camila? Her brothers won't let him have her. They'll kill him!"

His dark, brooding eyes filled his face and drilled into mine.

I looked at him, feeling downhearted. Nodded my head in agreement.

"But ..." I had to tell him about Ana.

"What?" He whipped around toward me.

"Ana is ... was ..." I cleared my throat.

"Ana? You mean your massage therapist?" He asked, a frown forming between his brows.

"Yes. She told me she was also having an affair with John."

Manuel stared at me; the left side of his mouth curled up in disbelief.

"Just yesterday. We took late *comida* together. She knows about Camila, too."

"What is that guy thinking?" He asked rhetorically as he allowed himself to fall back into his chair, as though thrown into it like a large sack of potatoes.

I shook my head back and forth, wondering the same thing.

We both stayed with our own thoughts for a bit, staring down at his desk, as if answers could be found on its gleaming surface. Then, Manuel stood.

"Well, can't do anything now, Carlita. Let's go listen to *música*. We need cheering, and we need to keep our distance from this," he said, his eyes intense, eyebrows raised, face hard. Easy to see how he'd scared criminals into confessing back when he'd been a detective.

On our walk to the bar, I decided I should tell Antonio what I'd heard. Manuel agreed.

"And, Carli, let him do the police work, okay? I know how you get. That's *his* job, not yours!" Manuel said.

I agreed ...

Though, could Antonio spare a policeman for keeping an eye on a scoundrel on the off chance those brothers might take him on a one-way ride? Not really, but even scoundrels didn't deserve to die for this kind of sin. Deserved to be taught a harsh lesson, deserved to lose something for having taken a woman's trust and stomped on it. For killing enough of her spirit that she'd be weary of the next relationship, stunting her hopes, lessening her expectations. She'd likely accept less than she deserved.

But did he deserve death? Surely not.

Yet, something in me went cold when thinking of the possibilities for John Sullivan's future.

CHAPTER 15

F irst thing after leaving home the next morning, I headed to El Café. Not because I needed matcha. I'd made my own and drunk it on my rooftop terrace, as always.

No, it was to see who might be there, who might let slip some tidbits about John and Lisa, whether anyone knew yet about them possibly divorcing. And whether he was letting it be known about Camila now that he'd asked for a divorce.

To my surprise, the first person I ran into was my friend, Amy. She'd been in Dallas most of the time since just after Millicent Jones's demise.

"Amy!" I called gently to her because no lady yelled in a coffee shop, even if she wanted to.

She was third in line, a typical morning queue. Swiveling towards me, her smile stretched ear to ear.

"Carli! Come up here, *chica*!" She beckoned.

We exchanged quick hellos, and I gave her my order. "Grande matcha with oat milk, please," I said, offering pesos. She playfully swatted them away.

I then stepped aside, letting the line flow, and Amy joined me after placing our order.

"When did you get back?"

"Oh, yesterday, actually. We landed just before four o'clock, you know, that American Airlines flight?"

"Querétaro?" I asked.

"Yup. The very one." Said Amy.

"Why here so early, then?"

"Oh, I have a massage appointment with Ana." She lifted her eyebrows several times in quick succession, like one about to do something forbidden, a little sinful, even.

I laughed. "Yes, *that* would get me up, and into town the day after a trip, too," I replied. I kept to myself how upset Ana had been lately ... how she might have used peanut oil when giving a massage to a man who was allergic to peanuts ... Amy and Douglas lived in Los Frailles, just a 15-minute drive but a world away from Centro's noise and chaos. Their stunning home, with its picture-perfect gardens, had even made magazine covers. They were big on hosting parties, especially for Música Clásica Esencial, who brought both up-and-coming and famous classical musicians to town.

She reached out and gave me a quick hug. I hugged her back and grinned at the unexpected gift of her affection.

"What was that for?"

"Just happy to see you, Carli. And to be back here. Gosh, I missed it." She gazed around her as she said it, contentment all about her.

We got our drinks from the pick-up counter, then headed to the courtyard in the back where the music volume was lower, and chose a table under the covered portion of the courtyard.

"So, John Sullivan, uh?" Amy asked, as soon as she sat.

I chortled into my cup.

"What? You haven't even been back for twenty-four hours!" I exclaimed.

"I have my ways, you know that," she said, a Chesire cat smile lighting her face.

"So, you know about Camila?" I took a sip of my tea, relishing its earthy taste.

"Camila with her *cartel* brothers, you mean?" Asked Amy, fiddling with her cup. She glanced around and lowered her voice, leaning toward me, before adding, eyebrows to her hairline, "one of whom got wacked?"

I nearly spit out the sip of matcha I'd just taken.

"So, you know ...."

She smirked.

"It's a cold hard world for people like that, Carli girl. Can't really avoid getting rubbed out at some point, I say." She took a sip of her drink. The New Jersey where she'd been raised sometimes came out in her speech.

Just then, Luna appeared in the courtyard, a *Vente* cup with the top off in hand, steam rising from it in soft tendrils, and her laptop bag slung over her shoulder.

She stopped short when she saw us, mild surprise playing on her face. As usual, she just didn't come onto the patio. She made an entrance in a fabulous pair of L'Agence seventies style jeans that flared from the knees down, a bright red wrap top with flared sleeves, and to complete the near-perfect vintage look, clogs on her feet. That red top said, no, it screamed, with a fiery boldness, look at me, I'm beautiful and I'm not afraid to show it. Adored this about her.

"Are you two having a party without me? And, Carli, no getting away from you, *chica*, you're everywhere in town!" She said, a huge smile lighting up her face.

I stood to hug her, feeling cherished in her embrace, surrounded by the smell of her perfume, Aerin Amber Musk, which seemed to have been created just for her.

Amy stood and they hugged too. So we all hugged.

"Group hug!" Said Luna, laughing.

"And you, Amy!" She exclaimed. "You decided to grace us with your presence? *Finally?*" Luna's face changed into a fake offended expression.

"Yes, I did." Amy replied, smiling. "You know I missed you all. Douglas had stuff going on in Dallas and I," she spread her arms out showing herself off, her bracelets jingling, "was required as arm candy and brain power for a bunch of events. You know how it goes." Anyone else would think of this as a complaint, but Amy loved her husband Douglas, and she'd swim across an ocean to help him out.

"Ah, husbands. They always want something from the wives. I think I'll just stay married to my laptop for as long as I can," said Luna, tongue in cheek.

Amy and I glanced at each other and laughed. Everyone knew Luna was a sucker for a *guapo* (good looking) man. One day she'd fall, I felt sure of it. And I knew Amy thought the same.

"So," said Luna, never one to hold back when she wanted to know something. Or when she had something to share.

"So, what?" Retorted Amy.

Luna scanned the scene. The couple at the next table had been swapped out for a solo woman lost in a hardback book and clutching a *grande* cup. The odd passerby meandered through the courtyard, and a man and woman chatted near the street entrance, too distant to eavesdrop on us.

"Well, I just found out that John Sullivan has been flirting with one of my clients. Actually, more than flirting." She wiggled her eyebrows.

Amy's and my jaws dropped way south.

"WHAT?" We both fake-screamed.

The woman at the next table turned our way, so we toned it down.

"What do you mean? How do you know?" I asked, my hand frozen on my cup of tea. I reminded myself to breathe.

"Well, I was at her house for some work, and she had a photo of them together on her desk."

Amy's eyebrows couldn't have gone any higher if she'd had an aggressive eye lift. Mine most likely looked the same.

"No ..." Whispered Amy.

I simply shook my head back and forth, finding nothing to say.

"I bet that *señorita* wouldn't be too happy about it,"said Luna as she looked at me.

"Did you tell her?" I asked.

"Who? *La Señorita*? I don't know her. Why would I ...?"

I interrupted her. "I mean, your client. Did you tell her about Camila, that's *La Señorita's* name, by the way."

"Are you kidding? And be the bearer of bad news?" She sighed. "Plus, why would I want to stir up the pot? To make trouble and be blamed for telling her? You know, shoot the messenger and all that?" She shrugged. Then lifted her cup to her mouth and gulped it.

"Anyway, she was sad because he broke up with her. Told her he wanted to work on his marriage."

What could we say to this new lie of his?

I puzzled about what could be going through John Sullivan's mind. How could he be married to Lisa and cheating with not one, not two, but *three* women?

Luna noticed my silence and asked. "What? What's going in that head of yours, Carli girl?"

Amy and I glanced at one another. I shrugged my shoulders at her—of course we were telling my best friend ever.

"Luna? One word. Or rather, one name."

"Hmm?" She posed it like a question.

"Ana. And he broke up with her, too. That's who you saw arguing with him in the park."

"Shut up!" She said, slapping a hand on the table, which made it wobble, and gaining another look from the reader at the next table.

The three of us sat, our eyes bouncing off one another's like billiard balls with haphazard trajectory, each lost in a whirlpool of thoughts, the air between us thick with unsaid words.

CHAPTER 16

L ater that afternoon, Lisa burst into my shop, a whirlwind of energy, clutching four department store bags, and several plastic-covered dresses on each arm. That was a first. Normally, Lisa was a buyer, not a seller, often donating her cast-offs.

"*¡Hola Carli*! *¿Cómo estás?*" How are you.

While her lips spread into a smile, her eyes told a different story—a stormy mixture of emotions. No surprise, since John had dropped the divorce bomb on her just last night ... yet here she was, acting like it was just another sunny day. And here she was, selling her clothes ...

"Hey, Lisa. Doing well, and you?" My instincts tingled. Something was off about her.

Oh, just a wardrobe cleanse before I hit the stores in Dallas," she replied breezily, attempting to sound casual.

I motioned to the triage counter. "Let's have a look."

She settled on a stool, but a fleeting moment of sadness clouded her eyes, giving away her facade. And no wonder.

"Quite the haul you've got," I said, examining the silk St. John blouses.

"I just thought, why not sell instead of donate for a change?" Her voice was light, but the forced laughter that followed betrayed her.

"You made the right choice." My eyes met hers, searching. The unease was palpable.

"I'm thinking of a change, you know? Updating my wardrobe, making it more San Miguel since I live here now."

I nodded, though not entirely convinced. "These will sell well." I held them up, examining them one at a time.

She stood abruptly. "I'll go check my mail at La Conexion while you sort. Is that okay?"

I spotted Sofia on the other side of the store, busy with rearranging blouses. "Sure. Most of these should be sorted through by early afternoon. Sofia and Esme will help with pricing."

Lisa hesitated. "I'd like to sell them fast, but no rush. And, uh, thanks."

As she left, I noted the tag still hanging from an Emporio Armani dress. New.

Cleaning out her closet, indeed. Was it the possible divorce? Or she wanted to see what she could do about making John fall in love with her again? It would take more than a wardrobe overhaul considering his behavior of late. I sighed.

The rest of the morning went by without fanfare. Sofia went online to start researching pricing for Lisa's cache.

It bugged me that she was selling. She'd never done it before. She'd been here three years, so I didn't buy her reasoning about updating her wardrobe for San Miguel.

Just before *comida*, Esme arrived, and the three of us dashed to La Posadita—a stone's throw from La Parroquia—for rooftop eats.

Grilled fish scent wafted from the next table, mingling with the occasional clang of the Parroquia bells. Sofia slid her phone my way. On the screen, a crystal chandelier sparkled.

I gasped. "It's perfect for the entrance!"

"Juan can hang it tomorrow," Sofia said.

Esme leaned in, her eyes twinkling. "Looks bomb!"

"Yes! Totally sick!" Added Sofia.

My eyes returned to the chandelier photo, a radiant mesh-work by Juan, our local glass genius.

As Sofia and Esme high-fived, I dialed Juan. He could deliver tonight. "Your store will shine even brighter tomorrow, Carli," he assured me.

The only thing clouding my joy was Lisa's behavior. John demanding a divorce from her. The web of women under his spell. It nagged at me, like a mosquito bite in a hard-to-reach spot begging to be scratched.

CHAPTER 17

I 'd just locked my front door, the cool metal handle pressing into my palm, relieved that the long day that had included the Tuesday night jiu-jitsu class I attended religiously, almost, had reached its end.

After what had happened last year, I'd decided some self-defense courses were in order. Even if it made my family uncomfortable, including Manuel and Antonio. They felt that with new knowledge on how to physically defend myself, I'd surely look for excuses to use it. Silly.

At first, I thought the classes would be tedious, boring, just something I needed to learn to protect myself, but they turned out to be enjoyable and I'd made some friends, and even gained more fashionistas for my tribe. They loved Carli's Secret Closet, too, and we often talked fashion before and after class, sharing ideas amidst the smell of the familiar sweaty tatami mats.

I took a deep breath. The open clerestory windows in my living room let in the night air, which tasted faintly of coming rain. Dap, who wound himself around my legs as soon as

I'd opened the door, got a scratch behind his ears. His soft purring provided me momentary comfort. He'd been waiting for me by the door a lot in the past few days. It brought to mind my ambivalent mood of late.

Before I could figure him out, my cell phone rang and buzzed at the same time, doing a bit of a dance in the front zippered pouch of the Coach handbag I'd chosen to use today.

Adele. I frowned, surprised to hear from her at this time of night. We weren't as close as all that. Oh, well, let's see. I picked up, my fingers slightly trembling. I think I knew what she'd say before she said it.

"Hola, Adele," I added a smile into my voice.

"Carli!"

Her tone of voice made the little hairs on the back of my neck and on my arms stand up, and a cold shiver ran down my spine. "What?!" I replied, heart pounding.

"John Sullivan? He's gone!"

"Gone wh ..." And then, I knew. My hands shook. My whole body. An earthquake.

"Oh, no!" I swirled around in circles, scaring Dap who plunged under the couch, letting out a long, plaintive meow on his way. No doubt my distress affecting him.

"How?" I finally managed.

"Not sure, exactly. Antonio was with me, got the phone call, and flew out of here. I thought you'd want to know."

Had I caused this? Had I not wished the Cartel Brothers would kill the philanderer? And settle the problem for us all? Sí.

But, had I not asked forgiveness right after for having had the thought? Said a little prayer? Did you not hear me, God?

I walked to the couch and dropped into it like a sack of ... oh, I don't know, something. Something heavy.

"Carli? *Hola?*"

"Estoy aqui." I could barely get the two simple words out. I'm here.

"It's okay, Carli. Don't worry. They'll figure it out."

"How? I mean. How did he die?"

"Don't know yet but he was stabbed apparently," she said, her voice slightly shaky. She let out a heavy sigh. "All Antonio told me is that he was found unconscious bleeding on the ground and presumed dead, just a few doors down from a woman's house who he was going to see. A massage therapist, I think? Or maybe not." Another pause, shorter this time. "He had a lover, right?"

Oh ... Ana? Ana had snapped and stabbed him? I should have paid more attention to all that rage coming off her in waves this past Sunday. Why, oh why, did these things keep coming my way?

Surely, I wasn't being punished by God for not having stayed in New York with the cattiness and all that came with it, only to be faced with bigger problems here at home?

"Carli?"

"¿Mande?" What.

"Huh, not sure how to say this, but my sister works at the same company as Camila's older sister, Eliana. You know, in

Guadalajara ... And they've become good friends." A deep sigh came through the phone line.

"Oh?" This was the woman Manuel had once dated, one of the reasons he'd left the police force. Well, because of her brothers, but the brothers had appeared in his life when she had.

"Hmm ... anyway, since all the goings-on Antonio told me about, I was curious, and ..."

"And, what?" I asked. "Do you know something?"

"Well, first, my sister and I? We tell each other everything. She was in Mexico City with me for a day last week for work, and we had dinner. She told me then that Camila is pregnant. With John Sullivan's baby." She took a deep breath.

There you go. The worst outcome. Lisa must have done it if she'd found out. A divorce was bad enough, but him flaunting a baby in town? At his age? And leaving her because of it?

Had John told Lisa about the baby after I'd stopped listening at the restaurant? And was that why the divorce?

"How far along?" I asked.

"About three months."

It came to me then. The danger Lisa faced. What if the brothers wanted her out of the way so that their sister's child could inherit? He was well off, after all ... had been well off.

The money would take care of their sister and her baby. Had they wanted him eliminated, not only to get at the money through the baby, but so they could find a more suitable husband for Camila? A Mexican man. One of their own. Another cartel guy, one who owed them a favor, because otherwise, why would he want to marry a woman with a baby—a gringo baby—in her belly, money or no, especially they now made plenty of their own? And did they realize John had two other children, adult children, in Toronto?

Or maybe ... they'd planned to kill Lisa, get John to marry their sister, then kill him too so the sister and baby could inherit his money? They'd have easy access to it, then. Was this possible? I knew little of our inheritance laws. But, if it were possible, that's how I'd do it. The gringo wife out of the way, the gringo himself gone too, the baby and sister taken care of financially, what better outcome? But Lisa was alive, and John dead, so, no. This scenario made no sense.

What nefarious thoughts came into my head sometimes ...

Maybe his murder was just a street thief trying desperately to get what he could? Muggings, some fatal, did happen here after all. Or maybe, the cartel planned things the other way around. Kill John first, kill Lisa, then the baby inherits. They must not know about his adult children in Canada.

I had to get to the bottom of all this.

"Adele, I have to go, mi amor. Thank you for calling and telling me."

"No problemo, Carli. *No problemo."*

I hung up and immediately dialed Antonio, and when he didn't answer, I sent him a text.

Who did it?

No response. I called again. No answer. I sighed, my frustration growing like a simmering pot. I texted again.

Well? Qué pasa?

No response.

I called again.

"Carlota! I'm busy here!" It came out like a grunt.I sucked in air. No one, other than my parents, ever dared call me Carlota. Except Antonio, when furious with me. I could count the times he'd done that on the fingers of one hand.

"Well, *lo siento*, but really, someone I know is dead?"

I found that with Antonio offense was best when defending myself.

"And I'm here with my detectives trying to find out who, myself! I don't have time for my phone getting blown up. By you. And he's not dead!"

Antonio's breathing sounded liked forced air coming through a partially closed vent.

Oh, really? My heart slammed against my ribcage. "But Adele said ..."

He interrupted me; his voice now gentler, clearly having calmed himself. "That's what we thought, but the EMTs were able to just barely revive him and bring him to the hospital. He was bleeding a lot."

"From being stabbed?"

"Yes. I need to go. And he has type O blood. They bleed more than other people, but even then, he's bleeding more than he should. The EMTs didn't have any of that drug that stops people from bleeding out. Tranexamic acid, I think."

"Oh, no! And ... is he still bleeding a lot?"

A loud sigh came down the phone line. "*Sí*, they can't figure out why." I heard the chirp of a fob unlocking a car door. "Even though type O does bleed more than others, he still shouldn't be bleeding this much. Not with this type of wound." His car engine roared to life. "Hold on, switching to bluetooth." Seconds later, he came back on the line. "I mean, whoever did this stabbed him on the left and missed all the organs. Great news, except now it looks like he'll bleed to death."

"Oh ... but the hospital has that tranxac ... transact ..., that drug that stops bleeding, sí?"

"Don't have the whole story yet, but apparently he's still bleeding even with that. It was thirty minutes before they got him stabilized and to the hospital from when they found him. Not sure how long between that and the time he got stabbed."

I remained silent.

"He might not make it, Carli." He spoke gently. "I need to go and see if I can talk to him, if they'll let me." He no longer seemed in a hurry, and I felt his sadness.

I hated, hated, hated, that this sort of thing could happen in the place I loved so much, where I made my home, where my loving family lived and thrived, and had for generations. He understood how much it hurt me. He felt the same, I knew, which was why he'd entered the profession. Antonio felt compelled to keep the world around him, and his family, safe.

"And ... aww ... I just got the sign. He's, huh, *Sí*, he's gone." A deep sigh followed his pronouncement.

Neither of us said anything for at least a full five seconds.

"Oh ...," seemed to be all I could manage to say.

Static filled the line again, a white noise tinged with distress.

Swallowing through a huge lump in my throat, I managed to ask.

"Was it them?"

"Who? The brothers?"

"Yes," I replied.

"Doesn't appear to be. It's a botched stab job if I ever saw one. A sicario would have gotten it right. He'd have stabbed him on his right for one to get the liver, at least, or stabbed him in the heart, though, that's harder to do. But, Sullivan would have been dead on the spot."

"Well, if not a *cartel* assassin, then, who?"

"*No lo sé*, Carli." I don't know. He added, "I have a few leads. We'll figure it out," sighing deeply.

I sensed his frustration. Though I felt compelled to solve crimes that affected the stability of my world, he was expected to do it. To solve even crimes that didn't personally threaten his world. It was his job.

He often breathed the blood of dead people, had to face their murderers, tell the families. Because he often did not leave all those tasks to the detectives who worked under him. He never cowered from unpleasant tasks. He took the crimes personally on some level, and Antonio was one of those people who handled his own stuff. Sargento de Investigación or not.

I went into my bedroom, threw myself on the bed, covered myself with the silk-smooth dark-red cashmere throw I kept on it. Its warmth, however slight, served for now as a feeble attempt at comfort. I pulled my bio-father's photo out of the nightstand drawer. His eyes stared back at me, almost lifelike. I mulled over all I knew.

So, not those cartel guys. They were probably too busy dealing with their brother's murder to even think about doing this right now. Right? How did their brother getting wacked, as Amy would say, affect their own standing with the cartel?

Surely not Ana. I just couldn't see it. Just then, the rage in her eyes came back to me. And it had happened near her house ...

And not Lisa ...

Neither of them could walk up to John on the street and stick a knife in him. I simply couldn't picture it.

So, who?

CHAPTER 18

John Sullivan's body was still waiting to be taken to the morgue in Querétaro—something about a shortage of ambulances. The doctor told Antonio that it's possible that had the EMTs had tranexamic acid, he might have been saved. But even then, maybe not. He'd bled so profusely—for still unknown reasons—before they got there, that it most likely would have been too late even then.

I would have to reach out to Lisa because I felt certain that Antonio wasn't telling me everything. And I needed to do more than I had been doing so far or I'd never figure out who had killed him.

At this moment, I saw Ana as the responsible one. But then again, the *cartel* brothers were more likely to do something like this, were they not? Even though Antonio and Manuel said the killing had been botched? And Lisa. Was it true that a family member was always the most likely suspect? But the same was said about lovers—especially, angry, vengeful lovers.

There were times when a girl needed to go to the home of her heart, which for me meant the *hacienda*, its pull on me inescapable. And my *mamá*.

I drove slowly out of San Miguel, and as I got closer to my childhood home, tension evaporated from my body more and more with each mile. As soon as I turned onto the ranch road, I lowered all the windows to flood my car with fresh air. Country smells perfumed the air and I smiled.

Every time I stepped foot onto the land of my birth, even after brief absences, I felt the familiar embrace of my ancestral home. Here, the world felt kind and conquerable.

Both our family home and Manuel's stood as the original gems on this land, crafted by our great-great-grandfathers. They might not have been the largest of hacienda homes, but their timeless craftsmanship stood out. Aromatic gardens wrapped around them, breathing life and legacy into each generation.

As the sun blazed from the west, it lit up the front of my parents' house. Pulling into the drive, tires crunching the gravel, I spotted my mother on the verandah, lounging in a big leather chair, her head in a book until I pulled up.

She stood and waved, and though I couldn't really see her smile from here, I felt it.

"Mamá!" I hollered, stepping out and waving my arm wide as if I were ten years old.

"¡Carlota! *¡Hola!*" She met my shout with her own jubilant voice, stopping at the verandah's edge to let me close the gap between us.

We hugged tight, her gardenia perfume mingling with the tangy citrus and aromatic tarragon that lined the verandah.

"Mija, ¿cómo estás?" she asked, stepping back but still clutching my arms. Worry clouded her eyes—had Manuel or Antonio spilled the beans?

"Muy bien, Mamá," I said. But her penetrating look compelled honesty. "You know about John Sullivan?"

She nodded, a shared sorrow lingering in our eyes. We finally walked back to the spot where she'd been sitting.

She picked up her phone. "Tea, *mija?* And Maria's *pan dulce?"* She smiled. There was no rushing her. No confiding in her without going through the niceties first, so I'd have to let her do her thing with that.

"¡Sí, gracias!" I exhaled, my heart tugging even closer to home. Mamá grinned and texted Maria, our ever-present housekeeper. Even on her days off, Maria often couldn't stay away, though she did take those yearly trips my parents insisted on—from Mexican getaways to a New York adventure and even a Mediterranean cruise. As a child, she'd filled me in on her latest escapade while I nibbled on *pan dulce.*

In no time, Maria approached, carrying a tray filled with fragrant tea and the *pan dulce,* placing it before us.

"Have coffee with us, Maria." I said, as I stood to hug her.

"No, no, Carli, *gracias, perro no puedo en este momento, haciendo sopa."* I can't right now, I'm making soup.

"Ah, Maria, trabajas demasiado duro!" You work too hard. I said.

She laughed, kissed my forehead, and sauntered back to her favorite part of our house: the kitchen.

Mamá then smiled at me, but not at her usual wattage. Then, she sighed. Deeply. This wiped the smile off my own face.

"Mamá?" I asked, suddenly anxious about her.

"It's okay, Carlota, nothing that has to do with us. It's just that gruesome thing happening." She looked off into the distance as a deep sigh escaped her, then turned back to me.

"He was cheating, John. With more than one woman." She sighed, and took a sip of tea. "And I know that Lisa knew because she once confided in me."

This shocked me to my core.

"She ... she confided in you?" I hadn't known that Lisa and my mother were so close.

"Oh, it was by chance. *¿Sabes?"* You know.

"How?" I straightened in the wicker chair.

"We were at one of the concerts, and I saw her in the bathroom. I'd gone during the concert, not during intermission. And she was in there, crying. So, of course, I asked why."

"And ... and what? What did she say?" I remained frozen in my chair, mesmerized.

"She told me that her husband had been cheating on her and she didn't know what to do. She felt stuck."

This saddened me despite my dislike for the woman.

"That's sad, Mamá ..." I reached for her hand, and she reached for mine.

"She left something unsaid, though, I could feel it. When I pressed her, she said that a divorce was out of the question completely."

"But why?" This puzzled me. He was cheating with all these women, why not divorce him if it made her unhappy? I told Mamá about the conversation I'd overheard at Manuel's Eatery. Clearly, Lisa hadn't agreed to a divorce after I'd stopped listening considering what she'd said to my mother.

"She wouldn't say. She was very agitated about it, though." She shook her head in disapproval of the whole situation. "She burst into tears again just telling me that much."

Whatever her reason for bursting into tears in front of my mother in a public place must be disturbing. It wasn't what one would expect from Lisa. Especially the part about not talking. Perhaps she was good with gossiping about others, but stopped when it came to her own life?

Did this mean Lisa *was* guilty? No ... not necessarily. Surely, as his wife, she'd come out of this better than the mistresses, one of whom had said she'd wanted to kill him, to poison him. *Oh, Ana ...*

"Awful." I said.

She shook her head, lips pursed. My conservative mother with the joy of being married to a man who adored her, and only her, could never understand such behavior from a man.

My phone vibrated and I pulled it out of my bag. As if I'd conjured her, Ana's name showed up on the phone's display ...

CHAPTER 19

With all the troubles in town and with John having been killed near her house, I had to answer.

"Mamá, I must take this, *lo siento*." I'm sorry.

"Hola, Ana." I held my breath, wondering what would come next.

"Carli! Thank goodness. You heard about John?" She sounded out of breath and in tears all at the same time.

"*Sí.* Of course. So sorry. I'm sure you must be upset." I shot up from my seat, phone glued to my ear, my heart pounding.

Mamá stared at me, eyebrows raised, fear in her eyes. Fear I was getting involved. I heard Ana sniffling like someone in tears.

"What happened, Ana? Was it ... did something happen between you two? Did ... did you ..."

"You too?" she nearly shrieked.

I pulled the phone away from my head.

"I just think back to our conversation at *comida*." I said, sounding as calm as possible.

"That doesn't mean I did what I said." She sobbed openly now, and sounded whiny.

"No. It does not. But, did you?" I asked, holding my breath.

Only silence from the other end of the line.

"Carli, I need help, I think. I'll be arres ..." She sounded like a little girl. And the phone line died. Had she been about to say she was getting arrested? My friend!

"Ana? Ana!" Nothing.

I collapsed back into my chair.

Mamá remained silent, looking at me, eyes wide, sitting ramrod straight, looking like a proper lady, waiting for me to illuminate her about my conversation. Why couldn't my life be as simple as hers? Now, I had to tell her about this because she wouldn't let it rest.

"You know Ana? My massage therapist?"

"Yes, of course, I remember Ana. I went to her once, remember?"

"Oh, yes. That's true." I nodded.

"Is she alright?"

"No. I don't think so. She might ... she might ..." I took a deep breath. "Well, she'd been having an affair with John Sullivan. And he was murdered on the street where she lives—just a few doors down from her house."

"Oh!" My poor mother was unaccustomed to all this mayhem. She didn't watch the news and her whole world revolved around calm, loving people. Well, there were always the Lisas in the periphery of it, I supposed.

"And Ana knew about his affair with a girl whose brothers belong to a *cartel*. Including the one who just got killed. Had you heard about that?" My voice and my breath trembled. "So ..."

My mother's eyebrows rose to meet her hairline while her mouth opened a little. She shook her head back and forth slowly. Then, she reached for her coffee cup and sipped from it, slowly.

Then, I dropped the real bomb. "And it seems that the young girl is pregnant. Three months."

Mamá blanched. "No, *mija*. Really?" She put her hand to her mouth as she took in a sharp breath through her nose. Her eyebrows were now knitted together.

I simply nodded while our eyes locked together.

"I have to go to her, Mamá. She's a friend—she's been a *good* friend. I don't want to abandon her now ..."

She simply looked at me, glaring. She didn't like me getting involved. I got that I couldn't leave so fast, that the niceties had to be observed even if the world were to fall apart around us.

So, we remained silent a moment while anxiety and fear for my friend churned in my gut. I tried to think of a fast way to make my escape. Mamá, silent, leisurely drank her coffee, while gazing out at the fields that surrounded us, pretending everything was normal.

I took a last sip of tea, picked up my handbag and began to get up to leave. She finally spoke, but first assumed her serious-talk-posture, sitting with legs crossed, back as straight as if metal pins held it up, her chin raised, while she looked at me with a bit of haughtiness.

"Well, all that will pass, *mija*. You know that. It's best you stay out of it like Antonio and Manuel—and your father and I—want you to do. *¿Entender?"* Understand.

I gulped and nodded. She just didn't understand how I *had* to solve these murders. Just *had* to. Plus, Ana ... this was not a time to abandon her, possible murderess that she might be.

As if all this turmoil was behind us already, she said something that had me falling back into my chair because I could tell my legs weren't going to hold me up.

"What it seems might not ever pass, though, your father and I are beginning to think, is what is happening between you and Manuel." She took a sip of her coffee, leaving me on tenterhooks, my heart in shambles, my mind in shock. This was *never* spoken about. Never.

Breath held, I openly stared at my mother, mouth agape, cheeks on fire.

The sound of a tractor in the distance reached us, and a truck could be heard speeding on the dirt road that led to the back outbuildings.

But, in this small area of the verandah, one could have heard a pin drop, so deep was the silence between my mother and me.

"Manuel and I?" I finally asked, at a near-whisper level, as if clueless.

My mother half-smiled, half-laughed at my reaction to her bold statement of this forbidden subject.

The look on her face was that of Dap after licking every last drop of cream from the bottom of his bowl. In her case, the complete satisfaction came from having taken me by complete surprise.

What a curveball to throw at me when a murder needed to be solved. I would have to put this aside for now.

CHAPTER 20

On my way back into town, besides my fear for Ana, I felt out of sorts, listless, my conversation with *Mamá* dancing, and not gracefully, in my head.

I parked my car where I garaged it, and walked to Ana's house, a ten-minute walk away near Parque Juárez.

To avoid the place on the sidewalk where I knew John had been stabbed, I took a detour. As I approached her house, though, I saw down the block that the area still had yellow tape around it and a policeman leaned against a house right by it, looking bored.

I had never wanted my couch and Dap on my lap more.

The officer standing there, though, hadn't been so bored that he hadn't thought to call Antonio when he saw me coming. When he hadn't even looked my way. How had he known which house I was going to? How did he even know me?

Just as I was about to ring Ana's Ring bell, Antonio pulled up in an unmarked car, skidding to a stop inches from me. Another detective was in the passenger seat, but Antonio jumped out of the car and came around it so fast, it was as if he'd been propelled in front of me by an unknown force.

I jumped back from the force of his energy.

"Antonio! What, *qué ... what is going on?" The look on his face said it all. The man was livid.*

"Qué? *Qué?* What do *you* think is going on*?"*

I stood before him, my heart slamming away in my chest like the drum of a marching band, speechless.

"What are you doing here, Carlota?" The fact he called me Carlota pointed to the level of his anger toward me. Arms crossed, not moving a muscle except for the one jumping involuntarily on his jaw, he waited.

Gulping, trying to collect myself, I took a deep breath.

"I came to see my *friend*, Ana, who feels very scared right now, Antonio. That's all." I adopted my mother's sometimes haughty posture.

"Why? I'm running an investigation here and the last thing *I* need, the last thing *this investigation* needs is you interfering!" His face was as red as I'd ever seen it.

"Is she about to be under arrest?" I said as calmly as I could.

He ignore my question, but instead said something that scared me on Ana's behalf.

"I'm waiting for the search warrant to be able to search her house. Should be here any minute." Arrogant, arrogant, arrogant. I guess this was Antonio if full cop mode and I simply had never seen him like this.

The only way I would get into Ana's house right now was by being bold.

"Can I go in until you get that? She called me. She's very distressed, Antonio."

Either he didn't really believe her guilty, or he had an ulterior motive for allowing this because to my shock, he agreed.

"I need to search your bag and your person before you go in, then you have ten minutes. As soon as the search warrant gets here, you leave."

When he saw the surprise and embarrassment on my face and saw me cross my arms, he hesitated, then turned to the other detective, now standing next to the car.

"¡Llame a una oficial para que venga lo antes posible!" Call for a female officer asap.

I relaxed a little, but barely. It was as if Antonio didn't know me, as if we'd never shared all those dinners and lunches, had never concocted all those adventures on the hacienda as children.

In a minute or less, another police car made its way down the street and stopped behind Manuel's. A female officer, face severe, nodded at him. She had to have been waiting just around the corner. And it then dawned on me that they'd want her on hand while searching a woman's house.

His face like stone, he addressed her: *"Registra el bolso de esta mujer y cacheala."*

Tears formed in my eyes, but no way would I allow them make their way down my cheeks. Search my bag and *frisk* me? Who was this man? I no longer knew him.

I started to protest, "Antonio ..." but the look he gave me could have a stopped a fast-moving train so I said nothing.

The female officer put her hand out for my bag and took it with her to the car. She was in there for several minutes, while Antonio and the other police officer remained, arms crossed in front of me in such a way that we keep me from running should I get the idea to do that.

Shaking, I did all I could to keep Antonio from seeing it, and kept my eyes downcast so he wouldn't see the tears that now blurred my vision.

The woman finally came out of the car, and nodded at Antonio. "*Nada*," she said. Nothing.

He simply nodded in acknowledgement, then glancing at her, he nodded in my direction, his eyes hard. She approached me and asked that I spread my arms and legs wide. Mortified, my face blushed furiously. How dare he? How *dare* he? Here? On the street with neighbors surely watching from behind curtains? Humiliation and anger consumed me like never before. I'd never speak to him again. *Never*! No matter how much he begged.

She patted me down thoroughly. When she was done, she looked at Antonio and shook her head.

He looked at me with disdain in his eyes. It scared me.

"You can go in now, but as soon as I get that search warrant, you're coming out." He huffed. "And when you come out, you'll repeat your entire conversation to me. *¿Lo entiendes*, Calota Cano?"

I said not a word, rang the doorbell again, certain that Ana, shaking like a leaf had watched the whole through her Ring bell camera. Reaching for my bag, I had another rude awak-ening.

"No, the bag doesn't go with you.?" He sent the female officer back to her car with it.

Would I ever get it back? As if he'd heard my thoughts, he added "You get it when you come back out."

And with that, Ana opened the door.

CHAPTER 21

Antonio had taken Ana in for questioning after I'd been banished from her house, and they'd searched it.

What had they found? I'd wondered.

Our visit had barely lasted five-minute when the door was assaulted by a series of violent knocks, and pounding. The doorbell chimed in, its notes clanging discordantly, one after the other in a frenzied loop.

Before either Ana or I, both in shock at the aggressive intrusion, could do anything, the door burst opened, officers and detectives piling in and yelling "*¡Policía! ¡Policía! ¡Tenemos una orden de cateo!*" while a detective brandished it in the air. Police. we have a search warrant.

We both shot up from the dining room chairs on which we'd been sitting, Ana in tears, telling me her side of the story, when the female officer hurried toward me. "*¡Señora* Cano, *necesita irse ya, inmediatamente!*" You need to leave right now.

My eyes barely met Antonio's, but he at least had the decency to look somewhat remorseful. I understood why as soon as I walked outside. Manuel, holding my bag against his chest, was leaning on Antonio's unmarked car talking to an officer in uniform. Antonio had called him, no doubt, possibly the reason he'd looked somewhat rueful as he banished me. Manuel might have given him a piece of his mind for treating me like a criminal when I'd only wanted to visit my friend.

As soon as he'd seen me, Manuel had taken me into his arms, and I'd buried my face in his shoulder, doing my best to not burst into tears again. He turned my back to the officer for privacy, and whispered "*Vamos*" in my ear. Let's go.

He'd taken me home, but had not come in, saying he really had to get back to his restaurant. A crisis in the kitchen.

Ana hadn't confessed to me. Not exactly ...

Sobbing as hard as I'd ever seen, her face puffed up and red from so much crying, she'd told me that she *had* used peanut oil on John, but feeling immediately guilty, had quickly wiped it off him. She hadn't known what to think when she'd later found out that he had gone into anaphylaxis shock. She'd been worried that she'd played a role in it, but said she'd still been so angry that she almost wished it would have worked to finish him off.

Shocked by her words, by her continued rage, my whole body shaking, my psyche, too, I'd taken the plunge and asked her. "Ana, *querida*, did you have something to do with what happened to John?"

She'd turned sad eyes on me, but hadn't answered because that's when the police had burst through the door. But I had information I felt certain she wasn't likely to give to the police. Unless they coerced her, that is.

By the time Manuel had come back to my house yesterday evening, bringing a bottle of wine, I'd felt helpless.

Because after he'd dopped me off, still quite shaken by how Antonio had treated me, I'd wondered how I could solve this whole mess when I was stopped at every turn?

Yet, I didn't want to give up. In the end, I'd given my head a quick shake to dislodge that thought. No go. Manuel was right. Antonio was right. My parents were right. I needed to leave it to the professionals. Sigh ...

But. Could I? Wasn't it the right and duty of every citizen to protect their home? The town where they made their home? Where their families lived? Plus, since the *cartel* didn't seem to be involved, it wasn't as dangerous anymore. Right?

Then, for a brief moment, my thoughts had drifted back to the conversation I'd had with Mamá earlier in the day. Even though it been just a few hours since, it had felt like a million years had passed. Remembering it made my skin tingle.

Had it been real? Had Manuel's parents had the same conversation with him?

And had he known? It didn't seem so. Silently, we'd made our way to my living room, and sat on the couch, both of us gloomy as could be.

"Mi amor, he didn't really mean it. He has a job to do. He can't treat you better than others when it comes to solving a murder ..." He ran his hand through his hair, a clear sign of his nervousness.

I'd ignored him, but after a few sips of wine, we'd gone to the rooftop, the night air thick with the subtle fragrances of blooming flowers around my deck, and begun to speculate on the happenings.

Could he have been so ... so *normal*, after a conversation with his own parents such as I'd had with my *mamá*?

Not knowing for certain if Ana had done it, and Antonio not speaking about it even to him, we'd gone back and forth on who could have done John Sullivan in.

"It seemed Camila's brothers would have wanted John alive to marry their sister, to take care of her and the baby, him being the baby's father after all." I said.

"It doesn't work that way, *sabes, Ca*rli." You know.

I nodded, mining my brain for answers. But none came. Only impressions teasing my consciousness.

"What if ..." I began but found nothing to add.

"What?" Asked Manuel.

"What if, huh, her brothers really wanted John dead, and now they also want Lisa dead, then the baby can inherit, and they don't have to deal with a *gringo* brother-in-law?" I asked, my head hurting from trying to put this puzzle together. "I don't think they know about his other children who'd obviously inherit also."

"Except what happened to John couldn't be a *cartel* hit." said Manuel, speaking slowly.

I shrugged. He looked off into space, considering it.

Manuel stared at me; his left eye squinted up in speculation. A nerve, I'd hit a nerve. But if so, it meant the *cartel* would be going for Lisa now. And at this point, as far as we knew, they hadn't killed John. And if they hadn't, they wouldn't be going after Lisa. Or would they? The whole thing made no sense.

Manuel shook his head in a definite way.

"So far, Carli, there's nothing to show that they did it. Antonio is right. *Sicarios* don't miss."

My heart kerplunked in my chest.

Manuel had managed to catch up to Antonio in the early evening before he'd come to me, but all Antonio would say is that the doctors had finally confirmed that John Sullivan had not died from the stab wound itself, but because of his fast rate of bleeding. That type of wound shouldn't have caused this kind of bleeding, even in someone with his blood type.

The conclusion was that John had been taking, or been given, a drug that made him bleed more. His local doctor told the police that he hadn't been prescribed any such drug, so now, the forensic lab would have to figure out what it was.

The morgue in Querétaro was taking its sweet time to do the autopsy.

Meanwhile, from Josefina, whom I'd called this morning, I'd discovered that Antonio had several officers canvassing the area of the Los Mezquites neighborhood where Camila's family shared a large home.

They questioned neighbors, including Josefina and her family, hoping someone had seen what had happened to the brother who'd gotten shot. He'd been just around the corner from their house when he got hit.

But as I'd speculated to Manuel last night, they most likely were not guilty of having killed their own brother. *He'd* been the *sicario*, the one able to conduct a professional hit. But that did not mean that the two remaining brothers had not killed John. The two killings were separate, had nothing to do with one another.

Manuel had shrugged, in slow motion, his left shoulder only, his gaze unfocused into the distance, which meant his brain was working on what I'd said about the cartel possibly targeting Lisa now that John was gone. If they'd done it. Even if they hadn't.

We'd remained silent, the general noise of Centro reaching us in spurts.

A roof dog barked a couple blocks away, a horn blared on the street just below my house, faint music from a restaurant slash nightclub a block away reached us, general traffic noise droned in the background of it all. Noises that confirmed Centro as a living, breathing entity of its own.

Finally, without saying a word to me, Manuel fished his phone out of his pocket, and dialed a number.

He'd stood, raising his eyebrows, and nodding his head once to let me know he was on it. A few seconds went by before a faint voice came through his phone's speakers.

"Antonio, *primo*, you have a minute?" He'd asked. And he'd told him our fears about Lisa.

CHAPTER 22

Today, though, as my humiliating experience with Antonio began to recede in my mind, I felt determined to figure it all out, one way or another.

Until the results of the autopsy were in, until I found out what had happened to Ana-they must still be holding her if she wasn't answering her phone—it felt as if my hands were tied.

All I could think was that she must be the one. The idea that Lisa or the *cartel* brothers could be guilty suddenly took residence in the way back of my mind. Still ... Ana? Really?

I felt helpless. Still shaken by yesterday, I'd been cowering at home this morning, ashamed of myself for doing so, repeatedly dialing Ana's number. I'd told Esme and Sofia to handle things at the shop, that I felt unwell.

Dap had been glued to my side since Manuel had brought me home. I wanted to call Luna, but felt so confused about Antonio's behavior and by what Ana had told me, that I wanted solitude so I could work it all out in my head.

I wasn't getting anywhere at home, and began to feel guilty about leaving things in the hands of two teenagers, as capable as they were. So, like a good business owner on a business day, I headed to the store, putting aside the dirty business that lurked under the polish of my favorite town, my home. Thinking about it made me sad.

Customers trickling in and out, Esme, working along with me, asked questions.

And got no answers.

All San Miguel needed now was a teenager running around spreading rumors about the specifics of a murder, one not yet solved. No, she'd find out along with everyone else, and not before. Which didn't stop her from pestering me, of course.

"But, Carli, *por favor*, I need to know at least *something*," she whined, her fingers playing nervously with a pendant around her neck, as if her knowing was of great importance. Which it wasn't. It was just over-active teenager curiosity for the macabre.

"Esme, *mi amor*, there is nothing to know right now. *I* don't even know, okay? Antonio doesn't even know either. The body is going to the morgue. There. You can spread that rumor. This one is actually true, at least." I sniffed.

Frustrated, with all the poutiness a sixteen-year-old girl could muster, she grabbed some clothes from the rack we kept by the register for garments customers had decided not to buy after all, and went to hang them back up where they belonged. Without saying another word to me.

"Te amo, Esme!" I called out. I love you.

She turned back toward me, a slight smile playing on her lips. Esme's mother, my older cousin Yolanda—whom I considered a sister—made me feel even closer to Esme than to my other nieces and nephews.

At *comida* time, I felt a need to go home. The conversation I'd had with Mamá would simply not leave me despite two murders occupying my mind, and now that I was somewhat distanced from it, I recalled it in full.

Once home, I headed straight to the kitchen to make a cup of tea, and as usual, gazed at the Gonzalez family's garden out my kitchen window while waiting for the water in the kettle to reach the correct temperature.

Several industrious gardeners trimmed away at shrubs, trees, and flowers. Twice a week they came, leaving the place pristine and affording me a pleasant view with no effort on my part. A gift. Owning a successful landscaping company is what afforded them their luxurious home and the slew of gardeners who buzzed about the place so often.

I smiled. I knew the Gonzalezes fairly well, from Música Clásica Esencial concerts and after-parties. My mother belonged and so did Ramon and Aurelia Gonzalez. Plus, I saw them around town on occasion and Aurelia consigned at my store.

After Mamá had pointed out my attachment to Manuel, I'd only been able to sit motionless, my mind too floaty for any words to come to me.

"Te amo, Mamá—I love you," I whispered, guilt overwhelming me.

"Y te amo." She replied. I love you too.

Shame-faced, I stared at the table, unable to look at her.

"As I said, your *papá* and I were talking, *linda*—sweetie, and well, we are curious."

I glanced at her enough to notice her face had reddened a bit. Was she embarrassed, too? I said nothing, so she continued.

"Well, you see, we notice that you and Manuel still spend much time together. We see that neither of you make real attempts at finding someone to marry."

I opened my mouth to answer her, but she raised a hand in that 'halt' gesture. I closed my mouth and waited. But now, the color of my face surely resembled that of the crimson poinsettias that filled large pots all around us.

"We never talk about it, we realize, because we don't want to face the truth of it." Added my mother. The woman who had apparently pretended to not notice the situation between Manuel and me for all my life. Until this very moment.

"You see, *mija* ... well, you remember my *tío Enrico*?" She asked.

I nodded, wondering why she'd bring up a long-dead uncle right after talking about my forbidden love for Manuel. Memories of him rustled like leaves in the wind.

I met her gaze, as she sipped her coffee with an odd rhythm that held me captive, each motion a deliberate dance. "He married Sara, another far-removed cousin," she stated, pausing for dramatic effect. I strained, but my memories of Sara were even more fleeting—just brief greetings during Sunday *comida*, at an age when the call of the playground had been much more enticing.

She resumed, "Sara handled the honey orders. *Tío* Enrico was in charge of the honey enterprise then." I blinked, that detail foggy. "Their relationship soured quickly. Everyone could hear them arguing through the hacienda, and Sara, in her anger, sabotaged the honey business, sending mismanaged orders everywhere, something that took months to fix."

A lightbulb moment. "So, the real reason for our family's rule against cousin marriages ...?" I trailed off, shocked.

She nodded, her gaze piercing. "*Exactamente.*"

My fingers tightened around my cup, tension spreading from my knuckles, threatening to creep up my arm.

Mamá reached over and laid a hand gently on my thigh, regret in her eyes.

"*Mi amor*, we see two people who love one another. We see a couple who pretend something else because their families don't want it."

I said nothing, my whole being transfixed by her words.

"Carlota, I just want to know. Is it true? Do you love Manuel? I mean as a woman loves a man, not just as a cousin or a friend?"

What could I say? Which answer did she expect? We'd all danced around the truth of that for years.

I couldn't even answer her. My eyes, still on hers, teared up. I simply nodded, swallowing, my head moving mechanically up and down slowly at least a half-dozen times.

It was her turn to stare. Before we could go on, though, my father approached us from the front door. Automatically, I stood as he came toward me for a hug. One I distractedly returned.

It became obvious right away that he sensed our mood. He seemed to have known what my mother had brought up. These two, so often, communicated without talking.

But would we now discuss this openly, the three of us? My heart slammed against my rib cage, confused about how to handle my mother's acknowledgment of my feelings for Manuel, and my realization that my parents had discussed this with one another.

"Well, Carlota, you will stay for dinner, *sí*?" Asked my father.

In shock and wanting to digest what Mamá had said about Manuel before speaking of it out loud with them both, I'd declined, saying I had to get back to the shop before closing, a half-truth.

My mother, apparently as shell-shocked as me over what she'd said and my response, didn't protest.

We hugged, all of us gathered in a tight circle. My mother's perfume mixed with the scent of my beloved father. He'd been out on the estate and smelled of the earth, the stables, of the goat pasture, of a little sweat, of all things that meant Hacienda del Cielo Azul to me.

My love for them knew no bounds, but right then, I couldn't wait to leave them, to get away. To think. To get over my shock. What had my mother's pronouncement meant? I'd been too afraid to explore it all too deeply.

Now, my phone buzzed, startling me out of my reverie. Manuel. I held my breath. A text.

> an ambulance is finally taking John Sullivan to Querétaro tomorrow afternoon.

> why so long?! I thought he was already there?

> No, he wasn't. No se. Shortage.

> ?!?

> I know!

Well, at least they'd be picking up his body soon, and we'd finally know what happened. What had *truly* killed him. Or helped kill him.

And perhaps who?

After that, the last thing in the world I wanted to do was go to work. But, I reminded myself of my business commitments, and went to Carli's Secret Closet, rebelling against it most of the way there.

Interestingly, going to my shop would turn out to be the best I could have done to advance my own investigation.

CHAPTER 23

When I walked into my shop, all my resistance evaporated. Of course I wanted to be here. This space was my very own small queendom.

There was no reason for thinking that the afternoon would not proceed as calmly as the morning had. But, in late afternoon, while I was instructing Esme on things I wanted done if she could get to them between customers, Lisa came into the shop, the cloying scent of her perfume preceding her, looking haggard.

I guessed recent widowhood would do that to a woman, though in her case, I detected something more to it. Didn't know what, but something. Her energy seemed, well, not like her, but then like what, exactly?

Plus, what was she doing here less than forty-eight hours after her husband had died?

Sofia, who'd worked alongside me since the morning, glanced at Lisa, then at me, and me at her. We then both stared at Lisa, shocked to see her at this time when she would normally have been at home, grieving.

Her visit was certainly unexpected, and too soon for her to collect on sales from her consignments. Though, I had sold several of her pieces already since she'd insisted on discounting them way down. Those St. John silk sleeveless blouses and shells? All gone as of this morning. Even the pricier Armani dress, its rich fabric so luxurious to the touch, had sold already. A businesswoman from New York had bought it yesterday. It hadn't even graced the shop for twenty-four hours.

"Lisa! What a surprise," I said in greeting.

"Yes, I can imagine."

I'd called her to extend my condolences, but I repeated them here and gave her a hug I tried to feel. But, *nada*. Nothing.

Her whole body seemed to collapse, as if all the muscles holding her up had released, the puppeteer having let go of the strings.

I waited for her to say more. She clenched her right fist at her side—did she even realize? Her left hand held the strap of a Givenchy tote bag, tan, one she'd bought from me sometime in the past year. It still looked good, I noticed; she took good care of it. Tan leather tended to be high maintenance. One had to keep up with it, wipe it down after each use, and spot clean when needed.

"Well, I'll have to take John to Toronto soon, eh ..." She trailed off, her voice cracking.

"I know, Lisa. I'm so, so, sorry." I said.

She shrugged. We all got distracted by the windchime tinkling, announcing the arrival of two women, a light breeze following them in. Tourists from Europe, I guessed by their stylish, understated clothes. They'd have fun here.

"Hola, bienvenidos, welcome!" Called out Sofia.

"Hola!" Replied one of them, a huge smile on her face. She clearly enjoyed being greeted in Spanish, giving her a sense of belonging in our *pueblo mágico*. Magical village.

They began to browse the store while Sofia and I turned back to Lisa. Who still stood right where she'd planted herself upon entering—about halfway between the door and the register. She remained frozen in place, an iceberg; little action on the surface, but who knew the magnitude of the goings-on below?

"Lisa, I'm so sorry too. I heard about your husband," said Sofia timidly.

No response from Lisa. Sofia blushed, embarrassed at being ignored. I sent her an apologetic look.

She returned it with her own confused look, nearly opened her mouth to say something else, but instead inched away from Lisa and me. She pointed herself toward our two new customers, asking them if she could help as she headed in their direction.

"Lisa, how can I help you?" I asked, finally.

"Oh, well ..." Her face showed her difficulty in pulling herself out of her contemplation. Or shock.

I smiled gently and waited, my heart going out to this woman who'd just lost her husband. Though ... something felt off. A near tangible sensation, like the negative energy experienced when entering a room where people had been arguing, for instance. *That* feeling. Or did I imagine it because of my usual ambivalence toward her?

"Did you sell any of my things?" She asked, her tone of voice monotone, that of someone expecting to be told no.

"Actually, we did. The silk camisoles and the Armani dress went already. Not the rest, unfortunately, but they've only been on the racks for a little over two days. I'm sure we'll sell them soon. Especially at those prices."

"Ah, good. Since I have to, you know, go soon," she cleared her throat, the sound rough, reminiscent of sandpaper on wood. "I thought I'd come collect the money from anything that might have sold, eh."

She looked at me, her eyes like pools of agitated water.

I waited a beat before answering, my brain whirring as I tried to figure out what this might be about. Lisa Martin did not urgently need the kind of money she'd be getting here.

"Oh, when do you think you'll be going to Toronto?" I asked, certain it couldn't be soon since John's body had barely gotten to the morgue. It wouldn't be released from the morgue for several days, possibly a week or more.

Sofia came toward the register with the two women, some garments slung over her arm, fabric rustling. Apparently, they were buying without trying on because they hadn't gone to the changing rooms.

Lisa and I moved aside, like dancers in a choreographed move, to give them more room to navigate toward the counter, and to keep our conversation private.

Still holding tight to her tote bag, eyes downcast, Lisa replied.

"As soon as they release him."

"Did ... did they say when that might be?" I asked.

She shrugged.

"I want to be ready, eh."

"I understand," I said gently, my words floating and staying in the air around us, as if they had no place to stop.

The music changed tracks from upbeat world to a slow Latin beat. Lisa noticed, looking up toward the ceiling as if trying to find the source.

While doing so, she noticed the new chandelier—which dressed up the whole shop, by the way—and startled at it, like Dap when he'd spotted a bird.

"Oh!" She exclaimed.

I followed her gaze to the ceiling and smiled. What a great addition to the décor. So happy I'd bought it.

The next moments went by like an action movie scene.

Looking up unbalanced Lisa. She wavered on her feet, like a tree in a strong wind.

The Givenchy tote's strap, precariously hanging on her right shoulder, betrayed her, the soft leather sliding off before her fingers could grasp it. As it plummeted, the tote disgorged its contents, scattering an array of items across the floor, some clattering on the wood floor.

"Oh!" Lisa exclaimed.

We both ogled the contents at our feet, our breaths held, like children caught in a forbidden act, as if we both wondered at how *that* could have possibly made it into her bag.

"Need help, Carli?"

Sofia called from a few feet away where she was now helping a woman decide between a Magda Butrym and a Stella McCartney blouse. Even from where I stood, I could see the customer should choose the Stella McCartney based on the style and her shape.

Without looking Sofia's way, my eyes glued to Lisa's, I called out. "It's okay. I got it."

My eyes traveled back to the floor and the contents of Lisa's tote.

That niggling feeling I'd had about her? It roared back, echoing in my whole being like the thunder of hoofbeats of a pack of wildebeests across a plain in Africa.

CHAPTER 24

We both fixated on a boarding pass, right there on the floor between us. So close to me, I could read it.

Rio de Janeiro.

Passenger name? LISA MARTIN.

Squinting, I could see tomorrow's date on it. A morning flight.

My blood slowed, cooled in my veins. My eyes stayed on the boarding pass as if joined to it by an invisible thread. Confusion. Through a fog suddenly surrounding my mind, I heard Lisa.

"It's not what you think."

Instinct propelled me to my knees to pick it up. Yes, I'd read that right. Rio. Out of Mexico City. For tomorrow morning.

"Lisa?" I asked.

She raised her eyes to mine, having crouched down herself by now, assembling the other things that had fallen out of the satchel: a lipstick tube (Clinique), a small, rounded hairbrush; tube of mascara (Estee Lauder); tortoise shell compact mirror which had opened when it fell; house keys; a small notepad; two pens; a package of facial tissues.

Two women, crouching on the floor of a woman's boutique, gathered scattered objects. The most prominent item's significance was impossible to ignore, one that could have as much impact as a bomb thrown into the lives of several people.

"It's not what you think." Lisa repeated, as she grabbed the boarding pass out of my hands and put it back into her bag.

Her face looked the color of a ripe tomato, the ones sold still attached to their vines.

Anxiety grabbed hold of me. *Oh, sure. You have a boarding pass to Rio when you told me you're taking your husband's body to Toronto. For burial. Your husband who died just two days ago.*

My heart stuttered.

All the items now returned to the tote, including the *bomb*, we stood. It's as if a force beyond ourselves held us to our spots on the floor, neither of us attempting to move away.

"What about ... I mean, what about ...?"

She filled in for me. "Toronto?"

I nodded.

She sighed, anguish on her face, in her eyes, oozing from every part of her, the energy around her so thick, a knife could cut through it, I thought.

Meanwhile, over the sound system, Enrique Iglesias began to sing *Ballamos*, telling his lover to stay with him, to not leave. But Lisa was leaving hers after fifteen years of marriage, at least, at a time he needed her to take care of his end-of-life matters. Wasn't his death enough of a punishment for his cheating?

Lisa opened her mouth a few times, a fish out of water desperate to dive back in, but nothing came out. She shot nervous glances toward Sofia, who also kept glancing our way, clearly feeling our distress. The customer was also following her gaze, most likely wondering what was distracting her salesclerk.

"Lisa, come with me, into my office. Okay?" I crossed my arms, assuming a no nonsense pose.

She stared at me as if I'd just asked her to jump out of an airplane without a parachute.

"It's okay, and ..." here I whispered, "we don't want Sofia to hear." I slid my eyes toward Sofia and the customer.

Lisa, befuddled with my discovery of her boarding pass, closed her eyes, took a deep breath, gave me a look I couldn't interpret, then followed me.

"Would you like some water?" I asked as I pulled a bottle for myself from the small fridge in the corner of my office.

"Yes. Please."

"Here you go." I handed her a bottle and she took it brusquely as if wanting to be certain our hands didn't collide.

She'd plummeted into one of the chairs facing my desk. I, on the other hand, sat gingerly, unsure I wanted the *bomb* found in her satchel to go off, which, of course, it would.

"Well, it's like this," she sighed deeply.

I raised my eyebrows and nodded my chin toward her as in *go on, tell me*.

"John and I had a pre-nuptial agreement."

"Okay," I said. Wondered why it mattered now. "Many couples do that." I added.

"Well, this one's a doozy, let me tell you, eh." She twisted the cap off the water bottle, her knuckles turning white from the effort. She took a sip, almost forgetting to swallow as she dove into the story.

"He ... well, he has, had, a lot more money than me. He didn't want to share if there was a divorce, he said." She wiped the bottom of the bottle with a tissue she'd pulled out of her bag to get rid of the dampness, before continuing. "He'd worked too hard, and he'd given up a big chunk of money to his first wife."

She set the bottle on my desk, staring at it, as though contemplating the weight of what she was about to say.

"He wanted what money he had to go to his two children. So, in a divorce, I would get $10,000, that's it." She chuckled bitterly, looking away for a moment, then back at me.

"But, if he died, I'd get our house here and the condo in Toronto, and a lump sum from his savings, enough to take care of the upkeep of both for quite some time."

She leaned back in her chair, crossing her arms. "The kids, *his* kids with the ex, get the rest."

She paused, looking as though she were thinking of something of importance, her eyes squinting into somewhere only she could see over my right shoulder, until she finally added, "Which is quite a bit. Nothing for them to complain about." Perhaps she was thinking about how much that was.

"Ah. I see." I said. Except I didn't.

So, John telling her he wanted a divorce triggered her to want to go to Rio—but only after he was dead? Well ...

As if she'd read my mind, she addressed that.

"Of course, I never thought he'd die so soon ..." She blushed, but it could have been for any number of reasons.

She gazed off behind me again where three Anna Halarewicz fashion illustrations, all black and white with shades of grey like in pre-color photographs, the women in long, glorious, poufy, feathered gowns hung on the wall.

"Well, this whole thing, him getting killed like that has me riled up. I don't know what his children think, I mean, after he... he ..."

She gulped water from her bottle. *A person uncomfortable with lying, but who was about to do just that?*

I waited.

"You see, Carli, John asked me for a divorce not long before he died. Just a few days before, eh."

Tears came to her eyes; she reached into her now-famed satchel, I assumed, for a tissue. I stretched my left arm behind me, eyes never off her, picked up a box of tissues from the credenza, and pushed it across the desk toward her.

"Thank you," she said, reaching for one.

I must admit, I felt her pain. To be married to someone you love and having him ask you for a divorce must hurt even if you are Lisa Martin, queen of gleefully blabbering about the bad things happening in the lives of others. Had she known about the affairs?

"I'm so sorry Lisa," I said, meaning it.

No way would I disclose I already knew about the divorce, or how. She'd start looking at the walls of my office, at the vent above us thinking others could hear, which wasn't true here in my shop.

Things still didn't add up. He'd wanted a divorce. Now he was dead. She hadn't killed him. The pre-nuptial left her financially comfortable in the case of his death. Why flee?

"Lisa, why Brazil? I mean, now?"

She gazed beyond me again, perhaps peering into her own past.

"My father lived in Rio for many years." She looked around my small office, as if the walls could transport her to a different place, then looked back at me. "Died there too, and that's where he's buried."

She adjusted her position on the chair, crossing her legs. "After my parents divorced, he met a Brazilian woman, got remarried, and had two children with her. They lived just outside Rio."

She paused to smooth her pants, her fingers lingering on the fabric as she gathered her thoughts. "I visited in the summers for about ten years, eh." Suddenly, she chuckled, her eyes taking on a faraway look. "I even stayed for a couple years and went to school there, an international school."

Shaking her head as if to bring herself back to the present, she leaned forward slightly. "Anyway, I've kept in touch with my siblings. And ... well, other friends there, too." She picked at a nail for a moment before meeting my eyes again. She blushed, but I read nothing into it at that moment.

"Well, why not take John to Toronto, take care of the financial stuff, then go to Rio if that's what you want?" I uncapped a pen, and nervously tapped it against a notepad on my desk.

"His children knew. I'm sure they think I had something to do with him ... you know ... dying." Her face flushed. She clasped her hands together on her lap.

"Knew? You mean they knew about the divorce?"

"Yes, his daughter called. I was in our bathroom; he was in the bedroom. I heard him tell her that he'd told me, that it was done. If she knew, his son knew too. Those two are close." She took a deep breath, visibly trying to steady herself.

She sniffed, blew her nose into a tissue. Tears kept sliding down her cheeks in slow rivulets while she crumpled the tissue and set it on the table beside her.

Faint notes from the music playing within the store, the distant tinkling of the door chime, Sofia calling out what might have been a hello, all of it reached us, but in muffled fashion as if through a noise cancelling headset, but probably because of the extra insulation I'd had put in here, so I'd have more privacy from the shop while I carried out administrative tasks.

It also meant that no one in the shop could hear what was going on in my office.

"I'm so sorry, Lisa. I, I don't really know what to say."

She shrugged. What *could* I say? She seemed to mean.

Still, the Rio thing didn't make sense. And why would his children assume she had any part in it? Did they believe her capable of stabbing him in the streets?

"Why would they think you had anything to do with him being de ... dyi ... I mean, his death?" I stuttered for the right words.

"Oh, we never got along. I'm sure they were ecstatic about the divorce."

Her face puckered in anger.

"Ah ..." Was all I could say to that.

"What's your plan? With Rio, I mean?"

"Just go for a while, let things die down. All the paperwork I need to do can be done from there. I can access my share of his estate from there, from anywhere, really."

She ran a tissue under her eyes, dabbed at them. She seemed to sit a bit straighter, resolve coming back to her.

"But what about taking John's body to Toronto? Won't there be a service there?"

Her face reddened. Her eyes lowered. She shifted a bit in her seat, letting out a deep sigh.

"They can handle it. *He* wanted to divorce *me*? *They* hate *me*? They think *I* did something? Let them deal with everything, eh, that I might have dealt with otherwise. For once, I'm going to look after Lisa. I took care of him *for years*!"

Her voice rose higher and higher as she spoke. Anger sizzled in the air.

"And look where it got me!" She nearly yelled.

I looked toward the door. Had Sofia heard? Her eyes turned to mine, defiant, her face darkening. I recalled that she could hear very little of whatever was going on in here.

I put on a neutral face and looked at her as kindly as I could manage, despite my heart beginning to resonate like a base drum in a brass band, palms sweaty, as I gripped the arms of my chair.

No way could I believe the fiction of her reason for going to Rio. A piece of the puzzle of John Sullivan's death still hung in the air. An innocent person wouldn't do that, would she? I shook the thought away. We all grieved in different ways, I reminded myself.

Had she perhaps hired a hit man? Made no sense. How would a Canadian expat—a retired human resource manager, now Reiki practitioner and astrologist—know where to find one of those in Mexico? Or anywhere? This fast too! It's not something she'd have been looking for until John asked for a divorce ... or would it?

Chapter 25

S he stood to her full height, rigid, head held high. Securing her tote bag straps over her shoulder, she squeezed them tightly. She wasn't going to drop it again; her *bomb* would remain safe in its depths. She frowned at me.

"Anyway, Carli. I'm not changing my mind about this. I'm not under suspicion. I hope you don't say anything to Antonio."

By now, she'd come around my desk and stood directly facing me.

Close in front of me. Much too close.

I went to stand too, to be on equal ground with her, but she came closer still, her knees touching mine. Blocking me from getting up. My heart, in full flight, slammed against my rib cage.

I opened my mouth to speak, but nothing came out. I cleared my throat and tried again. Pretending no threat existed, I spoke, calmly, to buy time.

"But, why not? I mean ... like you said, you're not under suspicion."

Of course, I now knew otherwise. Because suspicion tinted all of my thoughts.

"No. But, I don't want trouble, either. And I don't want to be *stopped*."

Her eyes drilled into mine from her position above me.

My lips pursed of their own accord; my eyebrows rose. All I didn't like about Lisa Martin came back to me in one swoosh. Her requesting that I keep something from someone in whom I often enough confided, a fact she well knew, irked me. In a roundabout way, asking me to lie. For her. As if.

Gathering all my strength, I stood abruptly, which sent my chair clattering into the wall behind me. Lisa startled, but her eyes flashed with determination, nonetheless. Growling, she lunged at me. Her free hand shoved my left shoulder while her satchel swung wildly from the other one.

No. This wouldn't be a repeat of the last time I'd faced someone with misplaced rage. No!

For the first time ever in the real world, I put my training to use.

I deflected her arm with a swift jiu-jitsu parry, but she, with unexpected agility and strength, pivoted on her heel and threw a wild elbow towards my face. I barely managed to duck, feeling the wind rush past my cheek from the force of her strike. She might not have known jiu-jitsu, but Lisa clearly had raw, ferocious strength behind her. Our breaths now came in short, angry puffs, blending with the scent of that cloying perfume she always wore. It seemed absurdly out of place in this scene.

Regaining my composure, I seized the momentary advantage. I shot my left hand to grip her right wrist, pulling it down while simultaneously slipping my right arm under her armpit, searching for control. Our muffled grunts filled the tense air as she resisted, pushing me back with a power and resilience that took me by surprise. It seemed she was channeling her desperation into brute strength.

With gritted teeth, her lips curling back in a snarl, she tried to knee me in the stomach. A muted "umph" slipped out of her when I deflected her knee sideways, causing her to stagger.

Seizing the chance, I moved behind her, swiftly, and secured my right arm under her neck in a classic jiu-jitsu choke. The soft rustle of clothing and a choked gasp filled the air. She thrashed, her nails scratching, attempting to claw at my arms. Luckily I was wearing a thick sweater which would save my arms from looking as if Dap had suddenly attacked me. I tightened my grip, breathing hard, knowing that if I could just hold on a moment longer, she'd weaken. I could hear the creak of the bookshelf straining behind me.

Lisa had one more trick up her sleeve. With a heave and a guttural grunt, she used her lower body strength to propel us both backwards. I felt the shock as my back slammed into the bookshelf, the few books on it nearly falling out.

I glanced at the door, wondering if Sofia could hear all this. But my guess was that with the music playing in the shop, her being busy with customers coming and going, and the extra insulation in here, she wasn't likely to hear much, if anything.

Oddly, this whole time, Lisa and I had seemed to mutually agree to keep the noise down. I didn't want my customers to be alerted, and Lisa likely feared Sofia would hear and call the police. It was as though we were characters in a silent film, battling mutely.

Though dazed, I managed to shove her off me, and we both staggered back, breathing hard. I kept my stance low, waiting for her next move, every sense alert. If she came at me again, I would be ready.

Lisa's satchel, still dangling on her shoulder, strangely, considering our tussle, caught my attention, and my mind raced. Guns were illegal in Mexico, but what if she had one? What if it was buried in the satchel? As heavy as one was, it might not have fallen out with everything else. Had I heard a thud when she'd dropped her bag? The weight of that possibility was almost as paralyzing as her having attacked me. Her quite possibly attacking me again.

Lisa's wild eyes met mine, her chest heaving as she took in ragged breaths. Amid the chaos, there was a surreal moment where we both just stood there, two women in an invisible arena, waiting to see which of us would make the next move, if any. Sweat dripped down her face. I felt some on my own face, and my heart slammed against my chest, shocked at what had just transpired.

"You have no idea what's at stake!" Lisa rasped, her voice barely more than a whisper, filled with a mix of desperation and fatigue.

For a fleeting second, she seemed on the verge of lunging once more, but then her shoulders slumped, and a defeated look replaced her earlier fierceness. The satchel's weight pulled her slightly to one side, and she clutched it tighter, perhaps sensing my suspicion about its contents.

Breathing hard, I slumped into my chair, my eye on her the whole time, adrenaline pumping through me at the rate of an erupting geyser.

"What's at stake, Lisa?" I finally managed to get out, getting my breath back, every nerve in my body alive, bracing for her response.

CHAPTER 26

S he took a shaky breath, shaking her head, hand gripping the straps of her satchel.

In a strange twist, she moved back to the other side of my desk, and threw herself into one of the guest chairs. Fascinated by this turn of events, I simply stared at her, noticing that my mouth had fallen open. I closed it.

"Carli, my goodness!" She exclaimed, as if nothing at all had happened between us. She rubbed her arm, which I had twisted during one of my maneuvers, her eyes wide, uncertainty playing over her features.

Silent, eyebrows knitted, ready fists at my sides, mouth halfway open as if getting ready to bite her, like a tigress protecting her young, eyes squinting.

A trickle of laughter escaped her, but it sounded fake. As fake as the stuffed mice I gave Dap to play with.

"Come on, Carli. *Please.* You can't think I was going to hurt you. I was just ... I'm upset. That's all." She swallowed. Hard.

As if trying to swallow too large of a something, like, say, a whole grape, or a whole walnut.

Stunned by the change in her demeanor, I remained silent. My eyes riveted on her.

"My husband just died. Give me a break, eh!"

Give her ... give her a *break*? She'd just *attacked* me!

"You need to leave, Lisa. Right now."

I said it in a low tone of voice, almost lazy.

"Well, first I want your assurance that you won't say anything to anyone about Rio."

Her eyes twitched with doubt, but hope reigned in them, nonetheless.

She put her hand into her bag. Adrenaline coursed through me, readying me for battle. I supposed I could have screamed, but then Lisa could shoot me—if she had a gun—before Sofia could get to me.

And, besides putting her in danger, how would bringing Sofia in now help me find out what had really happened to John?

Because Lisa knew more than she'd told. Obviously. And I aimed to find out what that was.

"I don't plan on telling anyone. What do I know to tell right now, anyway? Other than you have a ticket to go to Rio. You're not detained here. No one can tell you to not go."

Would she believe that? Because definitely, Antonio would figure out a way to keep her here if he knew this. How could her distress be so great she didn't realize it?

She took a step in my direction, but then stopped.

"If you tell, I'll do ... I'll do *something* to you. For real."

She stood, her eyes looking crazed again. Her fists balled up at her hips, and she wore a snarl on her face!

I braced for another fight.

Just then, a memory. When I was a little girl, my mother had taught me to use honey to keep flies, and fruit flies, from going after peaches and apples when our kitchen was filled with baskets of them at harvest time, just waiting to be made into jams, pies, and other pastries.

We'd cover several strips of paper in a mixture of honey and water, and with a few drops of dishwasher soap. We'd then add a small piece of smashed overripe fruit to each, also covered in honey and dish soap, then place the strips all around the baskets of fruit that nearly covered the whole surface of the large working table in our kitchen. The flies always buzzed right over to that instead of to the apples or peaches. They went for the rotted fruit and the honey, and the dishwasher soap did them in.

Now, instead of fighting with Lisa again, I'd use *honey* to get her calmed down, to lull her into thinking things were alright. Then, get her out of my shop so I could figure out what to do next. Something was up. She might not have killed John, but she'd done *something*. What? And why?

A little bell went off in my head, ding, ding, call Antonio! But I swathed it away. *No need for him.* Because I wanted to *know*. So, I let go of the outcome and went with instinct.

I walked toward her slowly, making myself as small as possible so she wouldn't feel threatened. "Lisa," I whispered, looking into her eyes with as much compassion as I could manage.

"It's okay. You can go. No one will stop you. Not me, certainly. You're not doing anything wrong."

Except attacking me in my office. In what was surely temporary insanity, she seemed to accept my words as fact.

At the same time, I rested my hand gently on her arm. My eyes never left hers. I watched the fight drop out of them, like a curtain coming down at the end of a theater play.

Removing my hand from her arm, I stepped back.

She began to cry again, wiping her eyes with one hand while gripping the handles of her satchel with the other. I'd never again be able to look at a Givenchy tote bag without thinking of this moment.

Just then, my phone, which I'd placed on my desk, buzzed and dinged.

We both flinched, but didn't speak. Our eyes remained locked. She backed toward the door, then did an abrupt about face, turned the knob, seemed surprised that the door opened, glanced backward toward me, then left my office, rearranging her clothes and hair as she went.

I nearly collapsed into my chair, but no time for that. Oh, no.

CHAPTER 27

G rabbing clothes from the closet I had in my office, I donned a makeshift disguise, including shoving all of my hair into a hat, at the speed of a stage actor on the sidelines with ten seconds to change between scenes.

I peeked out my office door, and didn't see Lisa. Sofia's voice, talking to a customer, reached me from near the changing rooms.

I crossed to the front door quickly, not saying a thing to her. She'd seen me, though, if the hiccup in her explanation of which dress would look best on the customer was any indication.

I quickly looked their way and spotted the two dresses Sofia presented to the woman. Instantly, I favored the early eighties Carolina Herrera in Sofia's right hand. Its colors matched the client perfectly, and the shift dress's design would subtly mask her middle, which seemed to be her style preference.

I snatched up some oversized sunglasses from a display near the door and slid them on, perfecting my disguise. I dashed out, hitting the street just as Lisa turned onto Zacateros. I hurried to the corner, rounded it, then eased up when I spotted her ahead.

Where would I go if I'd dropped a *bomb* like she'd dropped on me? If I wanted to leave for Rio with no one stopping me?

I'd go home right now, get my suitcases, and leave today. Right now. Head to Mexico City and make the call to change my flight during the nearly four-hour drive. Made sense. Surely, she didn't believe I'd keep this to myself? But who knew what desperate whispers flitted through her mind in moments of panic?

In any case, the last thing I'd be doing is what I observed her doing now. She continued to walk away from Centro, each step purposeful, and onto Ancha de San Antonio and its heavy traffic. But instead of hailing a cab to go home to Las Ventanas or to a parking lot to get her car, she turned onto the street next to Café Monet, then into the alley behind it, where the path narrowed. She was entering the Colonia San Antonio.

Heading that way, she'd only find small *tiendas* and cozy eateries—no major shops. It was primarily a residential area, and perhaps she was visiting someone? Now? She pressed on without looking back. Just in case, I had my phone ready, prepared to feign a call. Yet she kept her gaze down, stepping carefully over the tricky cobblestones, rough around here. Her quick pace and downward gaze revealed her unease—she'd rather not confirm if I trailed her. But did she wonder about it?

Finally, she turned into a small cul-de-sac,where the distant hum of traffic and city life faded. It would have been strange for me to turn, too, so I stood sideways on the corner with my cell phone at my ear, the warm sun at my back, pretending to speak to someone. Standing this way I could see which house she'd go into in my peripheral vision.

She glanced my way without seeing me, but quickly turned when the door on which she'd knocked opened, a faint creaking sound reaching me. She smiled warmly at whoever was there and entered. Laugher reached me. Seconds later, a man's head, sporting a huge grin, popped out the door, looked both ways, stuck his head back in, and, with a soft thud, closed the door.

My heart stopped. What the ... ?

Who was *he*?

CHAPTER 28

No chance that I'd knock on the door and start asking questions.

So, I returned to my shop, all the while mulling over what I'd seen. Lisa entering a house. A strange man welcoming her with a grin.

I'd made up a story to Sofia about why I'd left the shop in such a hurry right after Lisa, and in disguise, no less. She hadn't believed me, I could tell, but what could she have said?

I wanted to tell Antonio what I'd discovered about Lisa, but he was so angry with me ... how to do it without him erupting at me again? No way could I go through Manuel. If he knew I'd followed Lisa, sigh ...

I busied myself rearranging a display of vintage handbags. Then, the door chime alerted me to someone coming into the shop.

Evening was just falling, and I'd begun to think that I'd best go home and sit on my couch with Dap. Maybe he would inspire me as to how to tell Antonio that Lisa planned to leave for Brazil tomorrow? Because, surely, we couldn't let her do that?

The woman who'd just entered caught my attention. She didn't fit the mold of my usual customer. She dressed very conservatively, and not fashionista style. I sensed her discomfort in the surroundings of my shop, and subtly straightened a handbag, trying to appear casual.

She approached me, her eyes darting around, like someone who feared being caught at something. She spoke low, and kept her hands clasped together in an apparent effort to steady herself.

"*¿Señora* Cano?" She asked. Her brow looked a bit sweaty, the kind that came from nerves and not temperature.

My eyebrows shot up and my heartbeat sped up. Who was she and what could she want? I placed a hand lightly on the register counter next to which I now stood.

I almost whispered in response, but caught myself. "*Soy la* Señora Cano." took a deep breath, stood to my full height, and pulled my shoulders back.

"*¿Podemos hablar en privado, por favor?*" She asked, her voice low but urgent. Can we speak privately, please.

Well ... after what had happened with Lisa in my office a mere two hours ago, I felt uncomfortable taking this woman back there. I glanced briefly in its direction, then back at her.

Sensing my hesitation, she leaned in closer. Her fingers lightly touched the edge of the counter. She breathed deeply and said, "*Tengo un mensaje para ti del hermano menor de Camila. Dice que sabrás de él.*" I have a message from Camila's youngest brother. He says you will know of him.

I clenched my hands into fists for a moment, then released them, my heart slamming against my chest while I contemplated this. *One of Camila's cartel brothers knew who I was? How?*

Glancing Sofia's way and noticing that she was occupied with that same customer, I motioned for the woman to follow me, and I took her into my office. I held the door open for her before following her in, and closing it quietly. Leaving behind the relative safety of the shop, of Sofia nearby, of another customer in the shop, of other people around, in other words. The music reached into my office, but just barely.

Immediately, I turned to her, and assumed a ready pose to defend myself. Just in case.

The woman didn't seem to notice. Instead, she took a very deep breath, clearly mustering the courage to say something of major impact. She once again stood with her hands clasped in front of her.

Her eyes locked with mine, "*Mateo tiene información que te interesa.*" Mateo has information you want. She glanced around my office as if she feared others might be there and overhear. She leaned in again. "*Sobre el Señor John Sullivan.*" About Mr. John Sullivan.

My eyes narrowed, the gravity of what she was saying penetrating me through and through. Speechless, my mind drawing a blank, my body frozen in place, I let her continue.

She pulled back slightly, crossing her arms as if to shield herself, all while watching my face intently. "*Dice que necesita tu ayuda a cambio.*" He says he needs your help in return.

She seemed to be gaging me to see if I understood this would be an exchange, not just him giving me information for nothing in return.

But what kind of help could the member of a *cartel* think *I* could offer him?

She said that the help he needed from me was not dangerous to me or my family, but that it would be of great help to the police. If I was willing, she was to give me the address of a house where to meet with him. Right now.

I paused, gazing at a framed photo of myself on my desk, taken on opening day of my shop. I looked back at her. Taking a deep breath myself, I took the plunge into the unknown. I told her I'd help. If I could.

She left and I immediately called for an Uber, which arrived in less than ten minutes. While waiting, I changed into a black turtleneck sweater, black jeans, and black boots. If I were going into dangerous sleuthing territory, I was going there in style, and dressed in a manner that wouldn't get in my way when it came time to defend myself. If need be.

I grabbed a black Epi Louis Vuitton bucket bag from the coat tree in my office, and left my shop, barely waving at Sofia.

The nondescript house was on a narrow street behind a main road. The knot already in my belly formed tighter when I got out of the car, and it was even more pronounced when I knocked softly on the door. It opened almost immediately, revealing a young man. Well-dressed, dark hair cut short, clean-shaven. He could have been one of my cousins, a university student, someone's son, nephew, loved one. He didn't fit my image of a thug at all. Especially not with the fear emanating from his eyes. My first thought was that he was too young to die. That he needed a new profession to keep that from happening.

He nodded and let me in, glancing around nervously up and down the street.

We stood in a long hallway with a living room that opened on the right, but we both remained standing by the door. I shifted from one foot to the other, casting a quick glance at the living room before our eyes met. I waited for him to speak first.

"Thank you for coming, Ms. Cano," he said in perfect English, surprising me. "I lived in the U.S. for ten years before getting deported back here. My father took me there when I was nine years old. While there, I spoke mostly English." He looked down at his feet for a moment, then back up. He almost smiled, a sad smile, one that said he wished he were back there now, perhaps?

"Look, there isn't time for niceties. I need your help, and I can help you in return. I can give you information the police want." He fidgeted like a schoolboy. How could this young man be a member of a *cartel*?

"But, why me? And just so you know, I'm not sure how I can help you in return." I crossed my arms defensively. I mean, what if his request turned out to be impossible for me to fulfill? And what if he turned violent when he realized it?

Mateo looked me in the eyes and began. "What I want in return is simple. It's for you to go to the police with what I'm about to tell you. I know your cousin is the detective sergeant and that your cousin Manuel was a detective, too, once." His eyebrows lifted just a notch, his lips curling in a sort of half-smile while his eyes looked triumphant at my shock that he knew these things about me.

I let out an involuntary gasp and looked around, my hand slapping over my heart. I needed a chair and *pronto*. He sensed it, and serious now, guided me into the living room where I nearly fell backward into the first chair I came to. He sat in a chair facing it and started in immediately.

"You see, it started with our *jefe*. He wanted my oldest brother to kill John Sullivan." He paused and looked away, like he was grappling with the memory.

Eyes wide, gripping the arms of my chair, I asked, in a voice I hardly recognized as my own. "But, why? What did John do to him?"

Mateo hesitated, licking his lips nervously, perhaps feeling guilty about betraying his *jefe*, his brother, too, but then he continued. "As you know, John was involved with our sister, Camila. Before he arrived on the scene, she didn't know it, but another *sicario* in our same organization had been about to propose to her." He paused again, his eyes meeting mine, and his look told me that something momentous was coming. "This other man, this *sicario*, he's our *jefe*'s nephew."

My jaw fell wide open, then closed with a snap as I shook my head in disbelief. Mateo nodded his head once very slowly, and I realized that John had been a dead man the moment he'd set his sights on *Camila of the Cartel Brothers*.

Mateo's voice lowered, almost to a whisper. "But then John swept her off her feet, promised her U.S. citizenship, and she didn't want to see that *sicario* anymore. And then ... she got pregnant."

My eyes widened even more when I realized what had probably happened. "Your *sicario* brother was ordered to kill John?"

Mateo turned sad eyes to me. In them, I saw the pain of the life this young man had been brought into, most likely pushed into it by his older brothers and by the poverty his family had lived in.

"Yes, but he couldn't. He couldn't kill the father of Camila's baby, especially after she told him she loved John and was planning to move to the States with him. He was a hard man, my brother, but he had a soft spot for our Camila ... he wanted her dream of U.S. citizenship to come true. He refused the order, and ... they killed him for it. Shot him in the head and twice in the heart. As you know ..." He swallowed hard, his eyes unfocused, looking off into space as if trying to erase the horror of it.

A cold shiver ran down my spine. "Why are you afraid? Why do you want *me* to go to the police? Why not go yourself?"

"I'm telling you this because they've now killed my other brother too. No one knows where his body is except the *jefe*, me, and the man who killed him. He's dead because he stabbed John Sullivan wrong and he survived for a while. That should not have happened because Sullivan could have talked before he died."

"How ... but how did your *jefe* know that John Sullivan didn't die from the stab wound? Not right away, I mean?"

He looked at me as if wondering how I could be such an innocent. "One of the nurses at the hospital ... she, well, she gives our jefe information from there when he needs it."

I stared at him, wondering all the while what it must be like to have spies at your disposal. Mateo gave me a rueful smile, then continued.

"The *jefe* got impatient that this man Sullivan was still walking around alive. As soon as he knew that the stabbing didn't kill him ..." He gulped before continuing. "The *jefe* expected me to finish the job. To save my family's remaining honor and to liberate Camila so she can marry the nephew of our *jefe*."

He ran both hands down his face, looking the most forlorn I'd ever seen anyone, the most desperate. The most resigned.

"And I ... I," He glanced down at his hands, clenched into fists on his lap, then looked back up. His eyes glistened. Leaning forward, he took a shuddering breath, his shoulders slumping. "I just couldn't bring myself to it. I have never wanted the role of *sicario*. Instead, I went into hiding. Here."

Sitting back, he ran his fingers through his hair. "I hope to be able to leave town when things calm down. Because me hiding out is the same as a refusal to kill. And it makes me a target ..."

Taking another deep breath, he looked away, seemingly gathering his thoughts, before locking eyes with me again. "So I want to turn myself in, but I know the cartel won't let me live if I'm taken into custody in the regular way.

"They'll find me and kill me. I need protection. I need your cousin, Antonio, to know the whole story before I turn myself in. Otherwise, the police won't let me talk long enough to get the whole story out right away and I'll probably get killed before I'm able to give it all to them." He leaned forward, gripping the arms of his chair. His eyes, desperate, pleaded with me.

The whole time, I'd been staring, just staring at him, rooted to my seat like a statue in a museum.

Just then, a loud commotion erupted outside in the front of the house. Both our heads snapped toward the noise. Shouts.

The revving of an engine. Mateo's eyes widened in panic. "You need to go, *now*!"

"Wait, I ..." My voice trailed off when he interrupted, his voice urgent.

No time! Go through the back door, there's an alley on the right side that leads to the street behind us. You'll come out next to a *tienda* on Insurgentes. There are taxis there. Go!" He hissed out the command, looking back toward the front door as if expecting it to burst open any second.

I hesitated for a fraction of a second, then made for the hallway. Just as I stepped foot into it, he rushed to my side and whispered urgently. "My brother's body is in the house next door to my parents. It's vacant." His words hung in the air while I bolted toward the back door, his desperate face the last thing I saw.

Several fists were now pounding on the front door. I dashed to the end of the hallway, through the kitchen, and out the back door. Just then, I heard a loud crash from inside. They'd broken down the door! My heart in my throat, my whole being shaking and in shock, I found the alley, and ran all the way to the busy street.

As Mateo had promised, I came out next to a *tienda*. There were many people milling about, including some around a busy taco cart and no one paid me any attention. I turned to glance down the alley, and heard the most chilling sound echoing from the direction of the house I'd just left. I wasn't the only one. Heads began to turn in that direction.

Gunshot.

For it to sound so loud from where I stood, they had to have taken him outside in the back. Why? Were they looking for anyone who might have escaped? Had they asked and he'd refused to say? And then they'd ...

A second gunshot.

CHAPTER 29

Tears threatening, barely able to raise my arm, I waived down the first taxi I saw, climbed in the back as calmly as possible. In no way did I want to be connected to that gunshot. I gave the driver my home address.

Mateo! My whole body shook at the thought of that young life being snuffed out like that, like he didn't mean anything at all, a flea, a bug on the ground, inconsequential.

Had he been killed? Because of his going into hiding as a refusal to kill John Sullivan? Did they know that someone had just been with him in that house? Did they shoot him for *that* reason? Would they now pursue me? So many questions all running over one another in my mind like bumper cars.

Not least of them was my wondering at how a clothing designer from a good family, educated at Parson's School of Design ended up being drawn into all these murders, this ... this mayhem.

And what should I do about the dangerous information I now possessed? And what would Antonio say when he found out I had, yet again, inserted myself into his investigation?

But, I decided, if Mateo had died for giving me the information, it would not be in vain. I leaned over and gave the driver the address for Antonio's precinct instead. He looked at me in his rearview mirror longer than necessary, but said nothing, making a quick U-turn instead right in the middle of Insurgentes, causing a car or two to honk.

I texted Antonio.

> I'm coming to see you. Are you at the station?

Staring at my phone, I prayed for a response. Nothing.

We pulled up in front of the station. I got out and my heart in turmoil, I entered the building. No need to worry about whether Antonio had received my text, or whether he was there because he was standing right in the entry way, arms crossed at his waist, legs spread out, mustache twitching as he worried his mouth around a toothpick.

We stood, me not moving at all, staring at him. He stared back. To my shame and some self-disgust, my eyes filled with tears. I looked around crazily to find a place for some privacy.

Antonio, noticing my dilemma, walked toward me, and I couldn't help but flinch. He looked surprised at that. But beneath that tough exterior, I saw his face start to crack and that's all I needed to start crying for real.

The toll of the last few days just came pouring out of me in rivulets down my face.

He took me into his office, sat me in a chair, closed and locked the door, and lowered the blind on the one window.

He sat on his desk in front of me, arms uncrossed, his face not as unkind as it had been the last time I'd seen him at Ana's.

He lifted his chin in my direction, indicating for me to start talking.

I brushed away the tears, wiped my nose on a tissue, and took a sip of the water bottle he'd handed me. Taking a deep breath, I told him what I knew.

"I just came back from seeing someone who sent a messenger to my shop asking to speak to me. I didn't go looking for this, *entiendes*?" You understand.

It felt important that he knew I hadn't gone looking for trouble, but that trouble had come to me.

He looked frustrated, but still not having said one word to me, he indicated with his hand that I should go on.

I disclosed everything to him. About Ana having used peanut oil after all, about Lisa coming to my shop, about the ticket to Rio for tomorrow morning, and her then attacking me and how I followed her to a house in San Antonio, and how a man had opened the door to her.

I told him about how a woman I didn't know had then come to the shop to tell me that Camila's youngest brother had asked to meet with me, and what Mateo had told me. And that I suspected he'd been shot as soon as I'd left the house where we'd met.

It came out of my mouth nearly all at once, my words tripping over themselves. The whole time, Antonio stared at me. As soon as I was done, he walked around his desk and picked up his landline, eyes downcast.

"Cano here. Go to the Sullivan's house and bring in Lisa Sullivan." He looked up at me then, but continued talking into the phone. "If she's not there, I might have another place you can check."

I nodded my head. Though I couldn't give him the exact address, I could show him where the house she'd gone into in San Antonio was located.

He hung up, then immediately picked up the receiver and dialed again. "Alvarez, Cano here. Go to this address with backup, at least five of you. More if you can gather them up. There might have just been a hit there. It's possible it's already been called in, so check on that, too."

He put out his hand to me and I handed him the slip of paper with the address where I'd met Mateo.

After he finished that second call, he made his way around his desk and sat on it in front of me again.

"Carli ...." He started, then let out a huge sigh, as if he were incapable of continuing. At least, I was Carli again, and not Carlota. A great improvement. I relaxed for the first time in the past ninety minutes. Had it really only been that long since that woman had stepped into my shop?

"Look, I don't know how to impress on you that you can't keep doing this stuff. It's not a question of if, but a question of *when*, you'll get seriously hurt. Again. *¿Entiendes? No estás entrenado en trabajo policial*, Carli!" Get it. You're not trained in police work.

I started to open my mouth to remind him about my jiu-jitsu skills, but he put his hand up to stop me.

"Yes, you know martial arts. *Sabes*. But it doesn't mean that you know police procedure and what it takes to get a criminal convicted. You could completely mess up a conviction without even trying, *amiga*. And you don't know how to get yourself out of situations like the one you just went through."

I looked at my hands down on my lap twisting around each other, doing it of their own accord.

"Antonio, if that woman had not come, I wouldn't ..."

He interrupted me. "If she hadn't shown up, it would have been something else. Plus, what were you thinking going on your own to go meet a man who is a known *halcón*?"

He looked so frustrated, he reminded me of when he'd been a little boy and hadn't been able to talk Manuel and I into doing things his way. It had almost always been two, Manuel and me, against one, him. My heart ached for him for moment, but just a moment.

He shook himself off and stood to his full height, almost as if he'd just realized that him lecturing me wasn't going to solve all these mysteries. His phone rang and he picked up before the first ring had completed.

"Cano." He listened, then looked up at me.

"I'll meet you out front. Get a plainclothes car and ask for backup. I have someone who can take us where she might be."

I stood, having understood immediately what he needed from me.

In less than fifteen minutes, we were parked in front of the house into which Lisa had gone earlier. Before I knew it, there were six officers standing at the door, one ringing the bell, one shouting "*Policia!*" and Antonio had his gun pulled.

I saw all this from the back of the unmarked car that Antonio and another detective and I had ridden in.

The door opened from the inside, but I couldn't see what was happening from where I sat. Ten minutes later, Lisa was taken out in handcuffs, looking around wildly, a woman shocked by the turn of events. I made myself as small as I possibly could in the rear seat while still being able to see what was going on outside.

Less than a minute later, a man was taken out, also in handcuffs, and placed in the back of a different police car. It was the man I'd seen briefly earlier, the one who had opened the door to Lisa and had had such a huge smile on his face. He wasn't smiling now ...

All of this going on, but we still didn't know what had killed John Sullivan and who. Not exactly. We were still in the dark about what he had been given to make him bleed. And who had given it to him.

Just because Lisa had a ticket to go to Rio didn't make her guilty of anything. And just because Ana had rubbed peanut oil on him didn't mean it had anything to do with him bleeding so profusely. Peanut oil didn't cause excess bleeding.

A major migraine threatened to explode in my head, but I took deep breaths and calmed myself as a measure to avoid it.

How could I not think, though, headache or not, how one man's philandering had been responsible for so much turmoil and mayhem, and at least three deaths, possibly four, including his own?

Antonio and the other detective drove me home. They both came in to sweep the place for any signs of danger. Despite the tension that had been hanging between us the past few days, this gesture struck a deep chord within me. I guessed that Antonio still loved me enough, despite his anger, to ensure my safety. My heart swelled at the thought.

Would he contact Manuel now? Most likely, but the exhaustion from the whirlwind of the past two days overwhelmed me and I didn't have the energy to worry about it.

I headed straight for my bedroom, barely pausing to kick off my shoes. I lay down, Dap leapt onto the bed, nestled beside me, and began to purr, his engine-like hum the last sound I heard before surrendering to a deep sleep.

It would be ten hours before I woke up.

CHAPTER 30

ALMOST TWO DAYS LATER

Luna and Amy leaned forward in their chairs, their eyes like those in a Margaret Keane painting. Behind them, the Parroquia loomed over the moment. They'd come, summoned on this beautiful late Saturday morning with no prodding on my part, as soon as Antonio said I could tell them the whole story.

But we were on my rooftop, and before I could even open my mouth, the church bells went off in the somber manner of a funeral, just in time to provide an exclamation point to what I was about to tell them.

The biggest news was about how the middle brother in the *Camila of the Cartel Brothers* triangle *had* killed John Sullivan after all. Or, rather, partially killed him. His death had come due to two additional factors.

The brother's part in the murder was the botched stabbing. A substance he'd been given had finished him off, and even that might not have done anything, except for the fact that he had type O blood, which has an increased bleeding tendency. So, I explained to them, three things had killed John. Stabbing, aspirin, and his blood type.

"Wait. *What*!!" Cried out Luna.

I looked at her, pretending confusion and innocence.

"Come on! No way can aspirin kill you!" Added Amy, a smirk on her face.

"It can if you have type O blood, and your wife has been giving you six times the regular dose several times over. And when the member of a *cartel* stabs you on top of it." I shook my head at the memory of Antonio telling me that Lisa had confessed that to him after her arrest.

Amy slapped a hand over her mouth. "NO WAY!" She shouted. "*LISA*?!"

Luna simply stared, seemingly unable to comprehend such a thing. "What *loco* PEOPLE!" She exclaimed, fanning her face with her naked hand.

"Jeez, I'll say," added Amy, mimicking Luna with her hand. Which got her a look from Luna.

I chuckled, but soon stopped because there was really nothing funny about this story.

"But, wait a minute. I thought Antonio said John getting stabbed was just a street mugging?" Amy asked, cup halfway to her lips.

"Yes, he did. At first. But something I didn't know until later, the next morning, a neighbor who saw the stabbing came forward to give an almost-perfect description of Camila's middle brother." I paused, reached for my tea, and took a sip.

"That neighbor said she would have come forward before, but she was scared and had wanted to attend mass to pray about it, which she did that morning." Setting my drink back down, I took a moment before diving back into the story. "So, she went to confession before mass, and her priest encouraged her to go to the *policia* immediately."

I leaned back in my chair, looking up at the sky, searching for some semblance of meaning in all this mayhem. Luna and Amy remained silent, waiting for me to go on, lending gravity to the moment. I continued.

I told them, how, on the day they found John, Antonio and another detective had rushed to the Sullivan's home. They'd delivered the grim news, and apparently Lisa gave all the signs of being a distraught wife. But Antonio sensed she was hiding something. After he left, he got a chilling call from the hospital—John's wound shouldn't have been fatal. But something in his system had made him bleed uncontrollably. Antonio had said that his gut screamed Lisa, but he had to wait for the autopsy results.

"Wow, that's awful," said Amy, her voice betraying her confusion. "So, it took three things to kill him? Tough guy ..."

Sometimes, Amy could be cold ...

"When did they find out it was just plain old aspirin?" Asked Luna, her voice distant, dreamy like, as if in shock. Then, she sat straight up. "This makes no sense. If I took a ton of aspirin, I wouldn't just bleed to death. Doctors would give me a blood transfusion, and they'd have a drug to give me to stop the bleeding, *sí?*" She looked at me, expecting me to agree.

"Oh!" I slapped my forehead with a resonant thud.

"Sorry, I meant to tell you. They *wanted* to give him a blood transfusion, but he had O positive blood and they'd just run out and were waiting for a batch to come from Querétaro. Plus, people with his blood type bleed more, and longer than others."

"What? Why didn't you say so?" Asked Luna as she sat forward sliding her right leg under her left on the chair and leaning closer my way. "Even then ..." She added.

"Well, it wouldn't have mattered, they said he most likely would have bled that right out, too. They tried giving him tranexamic acid, which usually stops bleeding. But it failed."

"But why do people like him bleed more?" Asked Amy.

"Oh, Antonio says the doctor told him that they have less of something called the von Willebrand factor, something that clots our blood."

"Ah ..." was all she replied, looking a bit bewildered. She didn't really understand. Neither did I. Luna looked from her to me and back again, but just shrugged and said nothing.

Just then, car horns blared down on the street, louder than expected, even for Centro. Of course, this incited the roof dogs to start an impromptu "concert," adding to the chaos. We looked at one another, all stood at once, and walked to the edge of the roof deck, lining up like bowling pins, to peer over the railing.

"El stupido!" Exclaimed Luna.

Peering over the parapet, we saw a car stopped on the street. A figure in a long shawl, leaning on a cane, moved across the road, while another car behind honked loudly.

"People these days," Amy remarked.

We sank back into the soft embrace of our chairs, and I told them about Lisa having come to my shop early on Thursday. About her dropping her tote, about her ticket to Rio, about us fighting in my office, about the pre-nuptial, and John's children.

"Oh, my goodness, Carli! Such drama! How come you didn't say?" Exclaimed Luna, her voice rising in pitch.

Amy looked pensive, then asked. "When you say you had a fight with her, what kind of fight do you mean?" While asking, she poured herself some more coffee from the French Press and added cream and honey.

Her question got Luna curious, too.

"You know ... I had to defend myself." I shrugged, then decided to spit it all out. "Okay, so, she attacked me, so I got to practice ... you know ..." I trailed off.

"WHAT? Are you *loca*, Carli?" Asked Luna.

Amy, meanwhile, spoke right over her. "Wow, you, like, *literally* fought with her?" She shot up in her chair, back ramrod straight. "With that, what do ya call it again, Jitsu or somethin'?"

A smile escaped me. "Jiu-jitsu. I practice nearly every week. The only difference is that this time, I did it in the real world, that's all." I lifted my chin to them, shrugged, and pursed my lips.

"Aww ... Carli ... *te quiero*." I love you. Luna looked worried. I had to admit that if it had been her doing all these things—some of which she didn't even know yet—I would have worried about her, too.

"Y te quiero, Luna," I said to her, my heart filling with tenderness at my love for my best friend ever.

"Urgh, so mushy, you two," said Amy with a big smile, breaking up the moment. Then, she got pensive again.

"But that doesn't explain how the police knew about the brothers so quickly. The papers had it all this morning already." She eyed me with suspicion. Luna did the same, her gaze sharp.

"Ah, well, after I got back from following Lisa, back to my shop, I mean, this woman came in."

Both turned to me, at the speed of curious cats.

"I know ... it gets even wilder." They looked at me, expectant children equally eager and scared for what was coming next in a story.

I sensed I couldn't drag it out much longer. But, also, I felt it was time for stronger drinks and for food.

"Okay, I'll tell you everything else without stopping. But first, what about I get us a bottle of wine, and something to eat? I think we could all use it. Close enough to *comida, sí?"*

Both agreed, though reluctantly. They followed me downstairs to the kitchen where we assembled a platter: bowl of hummus, smelling of rich tahini and garlic, surrounded by mounds of juicy red peppers, crispy carrots, and celery. I opened a bottle of rosé wine, which released a fruity bouquet into the air. Amy grabbed the glasses, Luna the chilled bottle, me the platter, and we headed back upstairs.

Once settled, I continued the story.

I told them about how the woman who'd come to my shop had convinced me to meet with Mateo.

"¡*Ay!*" Luna blurted, putting up both hands in such a way that she could have stopped traffic on Ancha de San Antonio.

"You just ... met with a *cartel* dude? Alone? Seriously, Carli?" she gasped.

"Let her finish, Luna!" Amy snapped.

"Well, she takes too long," whined Luna as if I weren't there, shooting Amy a pointed glance. With a huff, she crunched into a celery stick, a petulant look on her face.

Amy smirked, clearly entertained.

Brushing off their antics, I refilled my tea. "The woman at the shop was sincere. I think she might've have even been his *abuela.*" Grandmother.

Neither spoke, both looking at a loss as to what to do about this habit of mine they called "putting yourself in danger, Carli."

Ignoring that, I told them about what Mateo had said about how both his brothers had been killed. And how it seemed he'd met the same fate minutes after I'd made my escape from our meeting point.

Their eyes, now filled with horror and shock, landed on me.

"After that, of course, I went straight to Antonio to tell him everything. And he took me to show them the house where Lisa had gone." I shook my head in wonderment.

"I watched them arrest her ... this woman we all know." I still felt bewildered by it, and Luna and Amy's faces showed that they felt the same.

Just then, my phone buzzed.

A text.

> I'm at your front door. Let me in?

> I'm with Luna and Amy. Telling them the story.

> I have news. OK that they're there.

CHAPTER 31

"Who's that??" Asked Amy, curiosity lighting up her face.

"Antonio, he's downstairs." I stood. "Going to let him in."

"Oh, good. Will we find out what happened after? About Lisa's arrest? About whether that Mateo is dead or alive?" Asked Luna, a glint of excitement in her eyes.

"Don't know, says he has news." I said this over my shoulder as I headed toward the staircase.

I left them there, the buzz of their conversation fading behind me, and went down to the main floor to let in Antonio. Things had not completely defrosted between us, but enough that we still kissed hello in the usual way. We immediately headed up to the roof.

"Antonio! *Hola*!" Said Luna, her voice bright, welcoming.

"Hola Antonio, *cómo estás*?" Amy greeted him, warmth in her own voice.

"Todo bien, todo bien." All is well. Replied Antonio, a bright smile transforming his face. I recognized the look as the one he usually wore at the end of one of his bigger cases. Satisfaction, pride, quiet joy at having made the world a safer place.

"Oh, you want wine, Antonio? I'm out of tequila." I asked, though I doubted it. Surely, he was still on duty, sort of, with three murders so close behind us, possibly four, and the weight of recent events hanging heavy between us all.

"Nah ... just some of that coffee you keep for Manuel." He raised his eyebrows twice in rapid succession to tease me about it.

"Why do you say it's for him? You drink nearly as much of it as he does!" I retorted, annoyed, though, he was right. Manuel was the main reason I kept Jamaican Blue Mountain coffee in my house, its rich aroma often filling my air when Manuel visited.

"Ha, ha." Luna said without humor, her voice flat. She knew.

Amy just smiled at me big, eyes dancing with silent laughter.

Antonio chuckled.

"Okay, y'all, stop it." The Texas slang of a youth spent at my bio-grandparents' home in Texas sometimes came out when I felt embarrassed.

I left them there to talk, but made Antonio promise none of the story would come out until I came back.

"Well, if you're worried, I'll come with you—he won't start without *me*," said Luna, giving Antonio an impish smile.

I stuck my tongue out at her, the childish gesture feeling both silly and comforting. As if he'd wait for her, but not me. Ah!

We headed down to the kitchen, where I turned on the kettle, the familiar hum of its heating element filling the room. I set it to two-hundred degrees, the perfect temperature for French press coffee. While I waited, I put two heaping tablespoons of coffee into the press, its invigorating aroma filling my nostrils. Antonio liked his coffee strong.

Luna sat herself at one of the three bar stools that lined one side of the breakfast bar, and once settled, went into the real reason she'd followed me down to the kitchen.

CHAPTER 32

As we waited on the kettle to heat up the water, Luna asked. "Chica, anything new about you and Manuel?" Luna probed, her gaze piercing.

I hesitated, recalling my recent conversation with my mother. Grabbing a cup from the cabinet, I placed it next to the kettle as delicately as if it were a fragile egg.

Luna's eyes darted between the cup and me, sensing my hesitation. "Why not try to talk to your *mamá*? You and Manuel are getting older. If you want kids ..."

I spun around, offended. "I'm not *old*, Luna! Sheesh ..."

"I just meant before you end up attending their college graduation at sixty!" she retorted, cheeks flushing.

I ignored this and summoning my courage, I murmured, "Mamá brought it up."

Luna's jaw dropped. "What? When? Why didn't you tell me?"

Seeing the hurt on her face, I went around the island and embraced her. We remained still, understanding the gravity of this new development.

"What did she say?" She whispered, as if discussing something sacred.

I felt the weight of her gaze. "Just that she noticed our bond, questioned my feelings for him." I frowned. "I admitted that I love him ..." saying this out loud felt like disclosing a forbidden state secret.

She tightened her hold, "Ooh, *chica* ..."

I extricated myself to prep the coffee tray.

Her eyes danced with joy for me, but what if nothing came of it? What if Manuel didn't love me in that way after all? How could I be certain?

"I don't know ... anyway, we better go back up before those two get bored and start telling tales about us."

Luna grinned, her eyes sparkling mischievously, and grabbed the tray from me. The soft scent of the coffee wafted around us as we headed up the staircase.

I followed her, my heart and mind full of Manuel. But also eager to find what had happened to Mateo, and what else Antonio might have found out from interrogating Lisa.

"Here you go, my favorite police officer," said Luna, sing song like, as she placed the tray in front of him.

"Your favorite? What about that detective, the one you flirt with every time you see him with me?" Asked Antonio, his eyes twinkling like stars in a dark sky.

I noticed that Antonio had noticed. Ah ...

Then, Luna blushed. I stared at her.

"It's just for fun." The sound of a distant mariachi band reached us. "Nothing there. You're my favorite because you're one of Carli's favorites; *inspector* and cousin."

"Huh huh," countered Antonio with a playful chuckle.

"Antonio? Who did you arrest? What happened to that boy, Mateo?" Asked Amy.

I looked at him and realized that the news he'd brought had to do with Mateo, and braced myself.

He nodded at me, sadness in his eyes before speaking.

"Unfortunately, he didn't make it ..."

Luna sucked in a breath, fist at her chest. "Oh ..."

Amy looked like she regretted asking the question.

No one spoke for a bit. I gazed at the spires of the Parroquia, and said a silent prayer for Mateo. Tears filled m my eyes, but none fell.

Antonio shook himself out of it, and continued the story.

"Well, first of all, we never would have caught Lisa Martin had it not been for Carli. She'd have been in Brazil by now, otherwise." He nodded in my direction. "I can admit it." He looked my way, an uncertain look in his eyes. I'd helped him, but by putting myself in danger, and he didn't like that part.

Both Amy and Luna nodded in acceptance. A glow of pride made my cheeks tingle and heat up. Though embarrassed by the attention, I felt pleased at his acknowledgment of my part in straightening out the mayhem of this whole thing.

Before he could continue, barking erupted from the street below. Two dogs clashing, their owners' frantic shouts of "Stop it!" mingling in the air.

The noise dropped, finally, and Amy, Luna, and I turned to Antonio as if our heads sat on the same pivot.

"Alright, I'll tell you, but only because we're done with the investigations. Since this morning." Antonio said, looking in my direction with an air of finality, as if he were the last authority on everything in the world.

I ignored his arrogance in favor of finding out what became of Lisa after her arrest, and to learn of Mateo's fate ...

He rubbed his hands together quickly like one anticipating something delicious other than the coffee. Still, he took the time for a sip of coffee, then sat back into his chair. Hesitated.

We all waited.

Then, he turned to me.

"Wait. Do they know about that woman who came to your store and what you did after?"

"Yes, they know all that."

"Do we ever!" Said Amy, shaking her head and sharing a look with Antonio that looked suspiciously like they both thought me crazy. Urgh ...

"And about Denise Bouchard?" He added.

I shook my head no. "I was about to, but then you interrupted by arriving." I chuckled at making him the culprit in holding out on Luna and Amy.

"Denise Bouchard?" Asked both my friends, almost in sync.

"Well, yes." I took a sip of wine and a bite of a celery stick with hummus.

Antonio smirked at my delay, while my *amigas* exchanged exasperated looks.

"The next morning, after all that happened, I got to thinking, you know."

"That's always dangerous," muttered Luna, raising her eyebrows at the others to make them complicit in her opinion.

"Heard that." I sighed in frustration. "Do you want to hear the story, or no?"

She put up her hands in defeat, gave me her best smile and blew me a kiss. "I'm just mad you didn't call me to do all that with you."

I tsk tsk'd at her, then continued.

"Anyway, I wondered who might be able to tell me about this man I saw with Lisa. I couldn't think of anyone at first, then Denise Bouchard, you know, as in Lisa's ex-best-friend—Denise-Bouchard came to mind."

The two women had been thick as thieves until Denise caught Lisa sharing her secrets with anyone who'd listen.

"I didn't want to just call and question her, and then I remembered how Denise often goes to the *biblioteca* for the Spanish lessons. But, what reason did *I* have to be there, huh?"

Luna and Amy's eyes sparkled with mischief, while Antonio's thumbs twiddled in his lap, his impatience showing. He knew this tale already.

"So, I played the greeting card angle. You know? The ones from the gift shop there?"

Amy chimed in, "Oh, by local artists? I buy those too!" and Luna echoed with a chirpy "Me too!"

"So, I went to 'coincidentally' bump into Denise."

Luna's laughter danced around us, while Antonio and Amy exchanged amused glances.

"And there I was, grabbing cards, even a gift for my cousin Alberto's upcoming birthday, when guess who's there?"

Luna grinned, "And you just 'suddenly' craved some of the *biblioteca*'s organic coffee and invited Denise to join you for a cup?"

I confirmed her guess with a nod.

"Anyway, we chitchatted about my shop, and about her up-coming trip to Italy." I took a sip of my wine. "I managed to slip Lisa into the conversation, wondering out loud if Lisa's gossiping might be a smoke screen."

Amy leaned in, "And? What'd she spill?"

Antonio looked at his watch, and poured himself another cup of coffee.

A phone buzzed, and Antonio looked down at his phone, nestled in an old-school cover attached to his belt. I wished his girlfriends would nudge him about his style because he never listened to me, the expert.

"It's Manuel." He said after glancing at his phone's display.

My heart beat a little faster. My palms felt sweaty. Though we'd spoken on the phone late last night, I hadn't seen him since my mother's revelation.

"Oh ..." I said.

Antonio looked at me a little strangely.

"Well? Should I tell him to come over?"

All eyes in the room focused on me.

"Of course!" I said, blushing at the attention and at the fact that three of them knew my reaction wasn't what it normally was when I had an opportunity to see Manuel.

Chapter 33

Antonio texted Manuel back, and put the phone back into its holder.

"So?" I asked him, nervous.

"So, what" He replied, pretending he didn't know I wanted to know if Manuel was on his way.

I glared at him.

He smirked, but told me.

"Says he's at El Café, he'll get you a matcha and come over."

Bless Manuel, who always got me a matcha when he could. But how would it be to see him? I felt as nervous as before my first dance at my *quinceañera*. As if I didn't know Manuel at all.

"Ah, my favorite *primo*! *He* knows how to treat me!" I said, grinning at Antonio. I wanted to keep them all oblivious to the new possible development for now. Except Luna.

"I know, I know. I'm just the one who gives you all the clues so you can have fun pretending to play cop." Antonio.

"WHAT?" I exploded. Sat forward in my chair.

"I'm the one who solves a lot of stuff *you're* supposed to solve because it's your job. Not mine!"

"I let you, that's why!" He retorted, eyes like spikes digging into mine.

"Let me? *Let* me? You're *loco*. You can't do without me in these investigations!" I recognized my arrogance, but was in no mood to take it back.

I pushed back into my chair; crossed my arms. And glared right back at the crazy *vato*. Dude.

My girlfriends watched, their eyes wide moving back and forth between us, as we volleyed words like tennis balls across a net.

The truth is that the police force was stretched thin—overwhelmed and overworked. They couldn't respond quickly enough. I reached faster conclusions because I also wasn't bound by their constraints.

Would they ever have solved this puzzle?

Definitely. In time. He was a very smart detective my cousin. But Antonio wouldn't have gone for Lisa until after the results from the lab came back showing an unusually large amount of aspirin in John's system. And those results hadn't come in until late yesterday when Lisa's flight would have been halfway to Rio.

And we only knew what we knew from Mateo because he had trusted that I would save his life by telling his story to the police before he turned himself in, but ended up getting killed in the process. I'd failed to save him ...

Plus, call it fate, call it luck, things like Lisa dropping her Givenchy tote in my store seemed to happen around me.

In any case, let's just say Antonio and I danced this dance; he told me to stop investigating, I ignored him, he then used the information I brought him. Then, he went back to demanding that I quit investigating. And I went on investigating, sometimes using information *he* gave *me*.

We both knew better than to take this argument any further. We enjoyed our friendship, and we were family too, after all, so we hung on to our unspoken agreement to never take this too far. Especially now that things between us were still a little raw after the other day at Ana's.

For now, I decided to go back to my story. No need to wait for Manuel. He already knew all this.

"Anyway, let me go on." I said, glaring at Antonio.

Luna sighed deeply, looking at us both with sadness in her eyes. Amy looked on the whole scene as if she were watching a movie, taking a sip of her wine and a bite of a carrot, her eyes never leaving us.

Antonio said not a word, looking down, composing himself instead. Probably his best move, considering.

"When I asked Denise if she knew whether Lisa might be hiding her own secret behind her gossiping, she gave me a look like she wasn't sure she should tell me something or not."

"Ooh ... what did she say, then?" Luna leaned toward me, interested.

"And I think she decided to tell me because of all the gossiping Lisa did about her last year."

"Okay, what'd she tell ya?" This time, it was Amy who showed impatience.

"She told me that when they were still friends, she'd suspected Lisa of having an affair with a certain someone, and that she wouldn't be surprised if it's still going on. Guess where the man was from?"

They stared at me, waiting for the rest.

"Brazil! So, the story of Lisa going there for her stepfamily didn't hold up, just as I suspected."

"Oh, so that means ... I mean ... was she planning something even *before* she knew about the divorce, then?" Asked Luna.

"Antonio, you want to take over? You worked the interrogation." I said.

CHAPTER 34

"O-M-G, Antonio! Carli! She was in a real interrogation room? At the police station?" This from Luna, who sat straight up and leaned toward Antonio as she said it.

Antonio and I turned incredulous faces toward one another, then to her. I mean, how else did she think the police got information from suspects?

"Sí. That's where we take people when we have serious questions." Antonio sat back, arms crossed over his chest, face serious, his detective persona on full display.

"Well, that hadda be scary for her, I'll bet," Amy threw in.

Luna, now deep into her chair with hands folded over her stomach, simply looked from her, to Antonio, to me, and circling around again.

Antonio nodded. I did too, slowly, trying to imagine myself in Lisa's situation. How very sad. And desperate. Wrong love made people do stupid things.

Pausing to take a sip of his coffee, Antonio looked at each of us in turn before diving back into the story.

"During the interrogation, she admitted that, because her husband cheated all the time, she gave herself permission to start an affair with a friend she'd met as a teenager in Brazil, Eduardo Gomez."

He set his cup down on the table. "They reconnected when he'd come to San Miguel for a vacation two years ago."

Leaning back in his chair, he glanced up at the Parroquia as if it held answers about the craziness of people, then looked back at us and continued, Luna and Amy hanging on his every word. Even me, who already knew this.

The couple had planned how best to pursue their relationship. He couldn't move to Mexico, or Canada, without the complications of obtaining residency, but Lisa, a Brazilian citizen, could move there. They both loved the ocean and the year-round temperatures of Rio.

The only issue, as Lisa saw it, was that Eduardo's financial resources in no way matched John's. And she wanted to keep the lifestyle to which she'd become accustomed while married to John. Why should she suffer? He'd cheated first and frequently. Had it not been for that, she'd never have had an affair.

The doorbell rang and I jumped up, ready to stretch, and dispel the nervous energy twisting in my gut at the thought of facing Manuel now.

"I'll be right back," I threw over my shoulder as I headed to the staircase.

I flew down to the front door and let him in, my heart beating fast. He balanced two El Café cups in his hands, while we cheek-kissed and hugged briefly.

A nervous tension like that of standing next to a high-powered power line sizzled between us. Instantly, I realized he knew.

"Carli, you look great!" He said, a twinkle in his eye, breaking the tension some. He handed me one of the cups. Matcha, of course.

Dap, who'd followed me, wove himself between Manuel's legs, meowing, Manuel being one of his favorite people.

I blushed. No makeup, and just plain Lululemon sweatpants and a thin hoodie, nothing fancy at all. Did he not like me when I dressed up? I mean, why a compliment over *this* outfit?

"Thank you. And you look *muy guapo*—very handsome—as always." I smiled, felt myself blush even deeper. My heart swelled.

Where were we going with this? Things I barely understood shifted inside me as usual when I found myself this close to Manuel. Except maybe now it was okay. Confusion reigned in my gut. Wait.

Had what my mother said now make it okay for me to feel this way about Manuel? I didn't know for certain whether his family had spoken to him, but it seemed like it.

Though, I saw no difference in his behavior, he was avoiding my eyes, and his energy felt different, hesitant.

Perhaps they had talked to him, and he didn't feel the same, so he opted for acting as if he didn't know.

And I was imagining that high-powered sizzle.

I shook off these thoughts.

"Well, come on up. Antonio is just telling the part about Lisa's interrogation."

"Ah, *bueno*." Good.

We reached the roof deck, and hellos were said all around.

The men greeted one another with a hug and some back-slapping as usual, and Amy and Luna also stood to greet him.

Once Manuel had settled himself into a lounger, his face up to the sun, eyes closed, Antonio continued with the story.

Lisa had mulled over how to handle the money thing. If she divorced John, her income would be too limited for her tastes, for what she'd become accustomed to. She wanted the same lifestyle she'd had with John, but to live it in Brazil with Eduardo.

She said that she didn't think seriously about killing John until he'd asked for a divorce, an event that changed things dramatically for her.

She'd realized at this point that, to get that same lifestyle with Eduardo ... John had to die. No matter how she twisted the possibilities in her mind, she kept circling back to John dying. That was the only way she could legitimately end up with what she felt was her fair share of his assets.

She'd hardly planned his murder, she'd said. Too anxious that he'd file a divorce before she could get a chance to figure out something else to do for money, she put a plan together quickly.

She had known that people with John's blood type bled longer than others, something that had sometimes been an issue for him. He'd always been careful not to cut himself, and once, he'd had to go to the hospital for just a paper cut that would not stop bleeding. There, he'd been given tranexamic acid.

Thinking about this over between the restaurant and home on the evening he'd asked her for a divorce, she'd wondered how to ensure that if John cut himself by *accident*, he'd bleed out.

From a mystery book she'd read, she knew that taking aspirin, lots of it, could cause bleeding that wouldn't stop. She'd started by giving him a whole bottle of aspirin that very evening. The next morning, she'd done the same. She'd managed this by crushing the aspirin and adding it to the smoothies full of supplements that he drank twice a day, one in the morning, and one just before bed. She continued to overload his smoothies with aspirin.

Only then did she try to figure out how to get John to cut himself, badly, and from somewhere he couldn't call emergency services easily. She hadn't had a plan for it yet when to her shock and surprise, he was stabbed in the street in Centro.

"Wow, that's quite the story," said Amy.

"What happens to Lisa now?" Luna wanted to know.

Antonio shrugged as if this were someone else's concern. "She's in jail ..." He trailed off, gazing into the distance. He sighed and added, "And there will be a trial, of course."

A sad cloud settled over our little group. The mayhem people got themselves into. But, also, satisfaction settled over me, happy to have had a hand in figuring out who'd caused all this mayhem in my favorite town where I made my home, where the family I adored made their home. Where many of my favorite people lived.

We disbanded after a while, all of us happy to go our own way. Manuel had been the last to leave, and when I" seen him to the door, he'd hugged me fiercely, burying his face into my hair, and breathing it in, sending my whole being into near meltdown, molten ore spilling into a cauldron. I so, so, wanted to let go, to give in to the embrace totally and completely, to lose myself in it and never return. To kiss him ... But first, things had to be figured out with our families. No sooner.

Tomorrow was *comida* at the hacienda, and we'd all agreed to go as a form of celebration about having put all this mayhem behind us. Manuel had offered to have a driver pick us all up and take us there so we could all indulge in champagne and tequila, as wanted, or needed.

We'd all consented.

CHAPTER 35

T he next day, in the early afternoon, the car Manuel had secured for us pulled up to the bottom of the stairs leading to the large verandah and font door of my parents' house.

As usual, before the car had even come to a stop, my mother had opened the door—as if she'd been standing at the window next to it waiting for us.

Mamá looked happy, her best smile pointed my way, which warmed my heart. I'd missed her even though just a few days had passed since our fateful talk; wished I could see her more often. My father came up right behind her, placed an arm over her shoulders, and both waved in welcome. They stood halfway between the front door and the edge of the deep and wide verandah.

I came out of the car and stretched, taking a deep breath, inhaling the air fragrant with the lemon and lime trees sprinkled around the front and side courtyards, the plumeria trees scattered around this portion of the property, and the Mexican tarragon plants that ran along the base of the verandah. The scents changed depending on the temperature, the breeze, and the time of year. I loved it.

Home again!

"Mamá!" I called out. She stood, ramrod straight while managing to look relaxed, waiting for me to go to her.

Always elegant, today my mother wore a sheath dress, this time one of my designs, which pleased me very much. As usual, her still thick and long salt and pepper hair was wrapped in a beautiful loose bun at the base of her neck. The tangerine silk of the dress complimented her skin tone perfectly; she glowed.

She wore diamond studs in her ears and the large diamond ring my father had given her on their fifth wedding anniversary. Considering its size, she needed no other jewelry.

"Hola, mi hija bonita,"—hello my pretty daughter—my parents greeted me. They spoke over one another, something they often did when greeting me. My heart warmed at the familiarity.

When I reached my mother, she wrapped me in a hug and held me there, the two of us heart to heart, not letting go, letting the moment linger. Were we both thinking of our conversation the last time I'd been here? Had it really been just a few days ago?

Papá, never liking to be left out, finally separated us to get his own hug. Because *Mamá* took my hand as soon as my father pulled me to him, we ended up in a group embrace. I could have stayed in their embrace forever.

We had to finally let go so they could greet Manuel and the others who'd come up to the verandah and begun to make noise.

We'd come early so we could bring my parents up to date on the goings-on with John Sullivan. We didn't want to talk about it in front of the few dozen uncles, aunts, cousins, and their families sure to show up for *comida*, the norm for a Sunday. Imagine the talk afterward!

Helpers worked at setting long tables on the verandah to prepare forthe meal. We all went into the house to let them work in peace (and to keep our story more private), gathering in the spacious living room.

Mamá went to find Maria, our housekeeper, but refused my help. They soon both came back, each carrying a tray laden with three coffee carafes, and two of chocolate to mix with it, or drink on its own, and enough pastry to feed a few dozen people, though there were but seven of us.

The rich aroma of freshly brewed coffee danced with the sweet undertones of chocolate, reminding me of morning treats from my childhood. The temptation to grab a pastry, with its delicate hint of almond and vanilla, was overwhelming.

Meanwhile, the smell of roasting pork reached us from the outdoor ovens just outside the kitchen in the back of house. No doubt, Maria, frantic to have everything just right had left the back door open to go back and forth more easily between the inside kitchen and the one just outside its door.

My mouth watered. Luna groaned in pleasure. "Hmm ..., smells *sooo* good!" She exclaimed.

Manuel stared at the near mountain of pastries facing us.

"Are you afraid of running out of *chiles rellenos* and pork loin? Is that why all these pastries now? We're supposed to fill on them before we get to the good food, right?" Asked Manuel, looking fake-offended at my mother.

We all smiled, and Mamá looked ready to answer him, when my father interjected with "The way you eat, *vato*, yes! We need some for our other relatives!"

We all laughed. Manuel did too, secure in the knowledge he never overate, and my father who loved him like a son, was simply teasing him.

"So, what happened with that John Sullivan?" Asked my father, as he sank into a couch, my mother close to him, both looking as if settling in for story time.

"Antonio will tell it," I said, as we'd agreed.

He went on to tell them all we knew, but left out the part where Lisa had attacked me, and where I had followed her to her lover's house. After what I'd gone through last year—something they did find out about—we'd all agreed to leave my part out of this story.

Before long, the rest of the relatives descended upon us. Many people had come today because of the great weather. The sun shone its blessings upon us from its perch in our vibrant azure sky.

Someone pulled out a guitar, two of my cousins brought out their violins, another a trumpet and the mariachi music began.

Every Sunday *comida* started with it, but it never lasted all that long. Once they tired of playing and wanted to eat, the sound system would kick in with more contemporary music, and they'd join in the conversations taking place all over the verandah, small groups forming here and there, gossip about family members, about affairs of the heart, and work complaints, all floating in the air below the roof above, keeping our family affairs from escaping on the breeze and finding its way to those who shouldn't hear.

By then, Manuel and I had each taken a glass of mimosa—we'd brought our favorite champagne and freshly squeezed orange juice with us—and found our way to one of two glider swings facing the house. We sat, silent, gazing at our families meandering along the verandah, and the grounds right below it, moving from group to group, sharing time together. Laughter, some outrageous gossip, inspiration, and always; love.

I noticed my mother looking at us thoughtfully. My cheeks felt hot as I once again recalled our conversation.

When she caught me looking at her, instead of the usual worried and anxious look when she saw any semblance of too much closeness between Manuel and me, she deliberately looked me in the eyes, then at Manuel, then seemingly at us both at the same time.

Slowly, she lifted her champagne flute with a gentle grace, in a "*Salud*!" fashion, her voice carrying the weight of a thousand unspoken words.

My father joined her and placed his arm around her shoulders. His smile looked tender, the kind that speaks of love and understanding, and he raised his glass in our direction.

Manuel turned toward me, the sunlight catching mischief in his eyes. He drew me closer, wrapping his arms protectively around my shoulders.

Manuel and I raised our flutes to our parents, and I felt the power of the moment. I latched my heart to the unspoken promise in the air.

Did it mean what I thought it meant? Was this it?

Just then, Manuel leaned to my ear and whispered, "*Te amo, mi* Carlita. *Te amo mucho.*"

Carli wants for everything to remain well in her world, sure. But, you know, life (and mayhem) happens ...

Cozy up with more Carli Cano mysteries—Just two quick clicks, and voilà – you're diving into your next amazing read at your favorite online bookstore!

When Music Meets Murder (Book 1)

When Mayhem Means Murder (Book 2)

Mayhem No More (Book 3)

Stitched in Deceit (The Prequel That Started It All!)

Got a print copy and eager to find all the links to the next books in one handy spot? Just head over to Carli's corner on my website – you'll find everything you need right there!

https://maryselaflamme.com/carli-cano-mystery-series

Loved the Book? Please be a Hero in my Story!

If you had fun with Carli and crew, the best way to support my work is by leaving a quick review!

Seriously—reviews are rocket fuel for indie authors like me. We don't survive without them.

I don't have the big bucks needed to plaster Times Square with ads, but I *can* reach more readers with your help.
Just a few words—no sonnets required (though I'd totally frame one if you wrote it).

Here's the direct link to leave your review:
https://maryselaflamme.com/review/

Your words help more than you know—and keeps future books coming.

Thank you from me, Carli, Manuel, Antonio, Luna ... and the rest of the fictional gang. You really are the cherry on top.

THE AUTHOR

Meet Maryse Laflamme—the *matcha-sipping, mystery-spinning, bone-broth-brewing badass* who turned a death sentence into a launchpad. At 71, she's living proof that reinvention has no age limit—from crafting compelling fiction in whatever corner of the world the wind last tossed her, to building an author empire powered by no-bloat blueprints and digital smarts.

She writes like she's talking to her sharpest, sassiest friend—and helps writers skip the overwhelm and actually finish their damn books. When she's not spinning worldly mysteries with grit, glamour, and just enough danger to keep you up at night, she's probably baking bread. Or taking a hike. Her voice? Irreverent, insightful, and infused with wisdom earned from a life well-traveled—and almost lost.

She made an incurable cancer her bitch, and came back armed with a pen, a plan, a story to tell, a vision to share, and zero patience for small talk or safe choices. And sometimes? She goes radio silent for no reason. Don't ask . . .

Dive Deeper into Maryse Laflamme's World! *Got questions, comments, or your own mini-mystery to share? Reach out through the contact form on her website. She's a reply wizard, unless you're sending Spam—then expect to be catapulted to the farthest reaches of the Universe!*

Stalk—uh, no, *follow* her online!

Here's where you can catch all her latest musings and clues:

Website: MaryseLaflamme.com

Facebook: Maryse Laflamme Writer

Instagram: @maryselaflammewrite

CARLI CANO MYSTERY SERIES BOOK 3 PREVIEW

MAYHEM NO MORE - CHAPTER 1

J ust when you think your life is now drama-free, somebody
drops dead at your feet.

I watched as my neighbor from the house behind mine, Ramon Gonzalez, walked toward me in El Jardin, San Miguel de
Allende's main square, his approach steady and assuming the
gait of a cat on neighborhood patrol.

I smiled wide at him. In return, he waved at me and grinned,
though I thought he looked a little peaked, as if he were a
painting that had started to lose its vibrant colors.

When he appeared, I'd been gazing across the square
at La Parroquia de San Miguel Arcangel—Parroquia for

short—the famous church whose pink wedding cake-like spires stood tall and proud, beckoning worshippers and tourists from all corners of the world, attracting them along with our beautiful UNESCO preserved town.

It was where my long-awaited day would take place, and quiet joy filled my heart as I gazed at it. Its spires seemed to reach as high as our perpetual blue skies and on up to heaven. Its bells would ring, their peals resounding like the triumphant finish of a grand symphony, to commemorate our happiness just ten days from now!

Seeing Ramon Gonzalez was a coincidence. I hadn't come here to meet with him or his wife, who I'm sure must have been close by as they did most things together, their lives as intertwined as the roots of old trees.

I stood from the wrought iron park bench on which I'd been sitting to greet him. We shook hands, then both sat next to one another. I scrutinized him. He ... well, he seemed different. There. More distant, perhaps? But no, there was something else ...

"*¿Todo bien*, Ramon?" All well, I asked him. Was he ill?

"*Sí*, Carli, *sí, todo bien*." He took a deep breath as if experiencing difficulties getting the words out. "*¿Y usted?*" And you. His voice faltered, and I noticed him gripping a handkerchief.

He didn't look or sound so well, as if a vacuum cleaner had sucked most of the energy out of him. But it wouldn't have been polite for me to say, so I ignored it, the same as I might overlook a tiny stain on his shirt so as to not embarrass him.

He wiped his forehead with his handkerchief as meticulously as if his life depended on it.

"*Estoy bien también. Gracias*," I replied. I'm also well, thank you.

Not wanting to bring attention to his flushed cheeks and the sweat on his forehead, I told him I was waiting for Manuel, that we were going to dinner to discuss final plans related to our wedding. We chatted about it, but I noticed his continuing shortness of breath.

He went on talking as if everything were normal. Said that Aurelia, his wife, was about town, shopping, and they'd agreed to meet here to grab a quick meal before heading home for a movie night.

He wiped his face again, and I wondered if now was appropriate for me to say something.

While deciding, I told him Manuel and I planned a long, relaxed dinner to cover all the last-minute details for our big day and honeymoon to follow a month later. Neither of us could get away for long right after our nuptials, though we had booked three nights in the honeymoon suite of a charming winery and spa just outside San Miguel. The thought made my heart beat faster, like a drummer's rhythm growing more intense during a song's crescendo.

Because we were sitting next to one another, my eyes weren't on Ramon the whole time, so it's only later that I realized I most likely missed some signs.

I'd been about to ask him if Aurelia meant to visit Carli's Secret Closet, the women's upscale designer resale boutique I owned and cherished, when he suddenly leaned forward, clutching at his chest.

"Ramon!" I exclaimed.

I watched, horrified, as his face turned pale, ashen, and he gasped for breath. It was a chilling transformation, mirroring a robust tree collapsing under a desert's summer heat.

"Ramon!" I couldn't help but repeat.

He fell quickly, his body folding in half, like a book closing. I reached out to him, to try to keep him on the bench.

"*¿Qué está pasando, qué puedo hacer?*" I asked. What is going on. What can I do.

He became very heavy, and I couldn't hold him up despite my best efforts. A man nearby made a move to help, but it was too late.

Ramon slid to the ground. His eyes turned glassy like a lively pond freezing over in winter, and saliva gathered at the corners of his mouth.

There were gasps around us, and a woman screamed.

My heart slammed against my rib cage, fierce like the waves that battered the cliffs of La Quebrada in Acapulco during storms. My whole head filled with the sound of it, obliterating all other noises, like that of the many people near us exclaiming, and calling out for help.

The way he looked, everyone could see that something awful had just taken place. He was as pale and still as a statue, his eyes glassy, vacant ... his chest no longer rising and falling.

No way to deny it. Ramon Gonzalez was dead. Right at my feet.

Continue to read Mayhem No More, Book 3 of the Carli Cano Mystery Series

https://books2read.com/MayhemNoMore